Beautifully
DESTROYED

BY

GRACIE WILSON

BLUE TULIP
PUBLISHING

Beautifully Destroyed
The Beautifully Series, Book 1
By Gracie Wilson
Blue Tulip Publishing
www.bluetulippublishing.com

Beautifully Destroyed

Life can take you by surprise, it can also put you through hell. My fate was never my own to deal with. It was ruined before I even had a chance. It was a rough start, and it hasn't gotten much better. Hiding behind the walls of my room is how I get through each day. Destroyed doesn't even begin to describe the way my life has been.

Finally, I get away and things are looking up. Of course nothing can go right and some things are just too much to bear. In comes the one thing I can't have. I've read so many books and I know the drill. Rock stars and musicians are not for me. I can't hide when they are always in the light. Something about him makes me want to step into that light, though. He is constantly bringing me to new levels and places I could never imagine.

The secrets I've tried to keep to myself are breaking into my new life. Having him around is helping, but the outside world ruins us as well. I either have to take the chance and let him in or push him away once and for all. Every time I pull away he is right back here pushing his way back in. He is relentless, he is everything I shouldn't have. Those secrets I tried to keep hidden begin to surface, bringing havoc to our lives. The world so desperately wants to keep us apart and I might just let it to keep my secrets.

Do I sit back and let the world pass me by or do I finally let those wounds heal and have the life he thinks I deserve?

Dedication

A fight against those who destroyed me.
A thank you to those who made me beautiful again.

"Sometimes it takes being truly destroyed to start over. Only then can you build again."

Chapter One

Fate

WALKING UP TO THE doors, my heart begins to pound as the hustle of the campus comes to life. Students are everywhere, lugging their bags out of vehicles in the expansive parking lot. Car horns go off in the distance only adding to the ongoing chaos of the campus. Students are finding the move-in staff who give them trolleys to bring their belongings up to their rooms, and they are all so excited. Not me. I'm doing this because it's what is expected of me. The University of Pennsylvania, or UPenn as they call it, is my new home. Harnwell College House, the place to start over. At least that's what I keep telling myself.

"Are you sure about this, Fate?" The voice of the only family I really have left speaks, and my heart breaks at the reality of this day. Clarissa was my child welfare worker. There was a time I needed saving, and she was that savior. "We can just get back in the car and head back home. You don't have to do this if you are not ready. You're only eighteen, you're still just a child." Her words ground me.

"We both know I haven't been *just a child* in a long

time. I need to do this. As much as I need to start over." My words bring a frown to the face I've grown to care for, no doubt hurting her. "Clarissa, I will call you every day, I will visit, and you can come visit too. This isn't goodbye." A normal person may get teary at this point, but I learned a long time ago that tears only cause more pain.

"Fate, I know this isn't goodbye, you're stuck with me for life," she says with a small smile. "I just wish you weren't so far away, is all." I grimace, and she holds her hands up in defense. "I know why you choose to be this far, and I agree, but that doesn't mean I like it."

I reach out and pull her into my arms for a hard hug and let the warmth of her embrace comfort me. She has been the only person I have let in or touch me in a very long time. "Well, no time like the present. Let's get you moved in, shall we?"

I just laugh at her fake cheer. I know she's struggling to keep her composure right now.

We unload the car, and I stand there with the trolley as she goes to park the car in the parent parking area. The hustling of the other families, some already saying goodbye, has my stomach in knots. Clarissa comes up behind me, and I push the trolley along with us. *Here we go, Fate, time to start again.*

Facing the door, I again glance down at my paper to double-check I have the right room. My room key feels heavy and cool in my palm. I insert it into the lock and turn it, opening the door and stepping inside with Clarissa right behind me. The room ahead of me is nothing extraordinary. It's a small sitting room with a couch and armchair on one side, a table with two chairs on the other, along with a fridge and microwave.

On each side of the room, bedroom doors face each other across a common sitting area, and a bathroom door stands open just off the back of the main room. Nothing special, but it's mine. Well, my roommate's and mine.

"It appears the roommate isn't here yet, so we get to pick which room. Which one do you want?" Clarissa asks joyfully. She seems truly excited for me to be taking this step, even though it will be putting some distance between us.

"Left side." Why I said that, I don't know, but something told me to go left so I did. Walking over to the door, I open it and the room is small. One single bed and dresser, a desk and chair, and some shelves. Nothing fancy. All well used, and that is completely fine with me.

Over the next few hours, we unpack all my belongings. My room appears exactly the way I thought it would. My bedding is green with white dots, and the wall decorations provide a nature theme. Just what I wanted since nature has always had a way to soothe me. Other than a picture of Clarissa and me, there aren't any other personalized effects.

"Does this mean I have to go now?" She stares at me with such sad eyes because we both know that time has come.

"It's time, but we should probably eat first," I say in a last ditch effort to prolong my time with her, even though it will only be for an hour more. I'm just not ready to let her go yet. She just smiles and leads the way out of my new home.

There are so many food options that it takes us about forty minutes to decide. We pick a little Italian place, but many others have been saved for when she visits me. Standing outside of my building, the night sky has slowly crept up on us. "Promise you will only drive for a few hours before you stop again."

Clarissa laughs and shakes her head. "I thought worrying was my job."

Smiling, I close the space between us and hug her as tight as I can. She returns her own tight squeeze. "If you ever want to come home just call and I will come get you." I nod into her, and she brushes her hand across the back on my head. "If you need anything call me, promise me."

"I promise." As she lets go and walks over to her car, a stir of emotions comes through the walls of my heart, but I quickly reinforce them. *Get it together, Fate.* These barriers are all that keep me from feeling everything; I can't even let the good in because the bad comes with it. She gets in the car, and the late afternoon sun catches the sheen of tears in her eyes. As she drives off I can't help the overwhelming sadness that takes over my body.

I stand there for a bit just watching the cars continue on their way, wishing I'm not alone, but knowing it had to come to this, so why not just get it over with? There comes a time when you have to just say, screw it, world, I'm here. Well, at least that's what my mom used to tell me.

When I turn around I continue to walk into my building and head to my room. It doesn't feel as exciting the second time I enter. It just feels lonely. The lights are all on. Thankfully, I thought ahead and didn't turn them off when I left. Continuing on to my room, I shut and lock the door behind me then plop on my bed. I'm exhausted, but I won't sleep. I can't. Not yet. So I pull out my computer and start looking into my new surroundings. UPenn is definitely different from anything I've ever dealt with before. When I'm done researching the college and Philadelphia, I pull out a book and begin reading.

Just as I'm finishing my book, the sun is rising. I get up to turn the lights off and gaze out the window. Students are still moving in today, and soon I should be meeting my roommate, Cameron. I dread this, but I'm also excited. Back home I didn't really have friends. Not after everyone knew what happened. So, I just focused on school and reading. Now I get to start over, so I'm hoping my roommate and I can be friends. When you apply, they try to match you up with someone who has similar interests so you are compatible. Hopefully, the computers are right because I could use someone to talk to here. Climbing into my bed, I quickly fall asleep in the brightness of the day.

BANG.

My eyes flutter open and I glance at my clock. It's just after one o'clock, and I've slept a good six hours.

Bang. Bang.

The noises coming from the other room are loud, telling me that someone's out there. That must be Cameron. I go to the door and open it to introduce myself, but I can't see her. She must be in her room.

I cross the common area and go to lean against the door. "Hey—" I yelp almost falling over at the sight of the man before me. I run back to my room and slam the door behind me. I've just made the biggest fool of myself. I glance down and catch sight of my pajamas, a small pair of shorts with a tank top. They're comfy and have little kitties all over them. I never thought to get dressed because I didn't expect her to not be alone. *Duh. People have people. Just not me.*

A quiet knock at my door startles me. I turn and crack it open. On the other side stands the most attractive guy I've ever seen. He has short dark brown hair, pale skin, and, from what I can see, a very well developed body. His eyes, wow they are the brightest shade of blue I've ever seen. The thoughts make my heart race and not in a good way. *Breathe.*

"I'm sorry. I didn't mean to startle you." He appears genuine and gives me a small smile. *God, he has dimples.* No man should be as handsome as this, and he definitely shouldn't be grinning at me the way he is. I squirm under his gaze, and for a moment, I forget I'm in my pajamas. When I gather my wits and remember, I quickly bring my arms across my chest. *Real smooth.* He tries to hide it, but he chuckles softly. I slink away from him, pulling myself farther into my room using the door to cover me a little.

"It's okay," I say quietly, trying not to stare at him. He puts a pair of earplugs on the shelf right next to my door. I give him an odd look, asking him to elaborate. Talking to men is not something I do. When he doesn't, I have no choice but to talk.

"She's a snorer?" I ask, hoping he's just giving them to me so that his girlfriend or sister and I don't run into any roommate issues.

Again, he chuckles. "Maybe…" he says, and I glare

at him in confusion. "Well, you must be Fate," he says, sticking out his hand for me to shake. I look to him and hesitate. *Time to be normal, Fate.* Taking a deep breath, I place my hand in his and shake it firmly.

"Yes, I am," I say with a shy smile.

"Great, that'd be weird if someone else was in your room, right?" he says with a chuckle. "I'm Cameron." My breath catches and I pull my hand away.

What…the…hell…

Chapter Two

Fate

"CAMERON IS A BOY…" Clarissa says from the other end of the phone.

"Yes, a boy. How did that happen?" I say in a panic. This cannot be happening. Me, living with a man. Well, that's just going to be an anxiety problem.

"I told you that box meant *Gender* as in co-ed living, not the sexual orientation of your roommate. But you wouldn't listen, you were all, 'I don't care as long as we get along.' Well, babe, the computers seem to think you will get along with Cameron…who is a man. Not a boy. Since the age on the fact sheet says twenty-one." From the mirth in her voice, she is enjoying this. I was determined to do this university thing and all the joyous paperwork alone. I didn't even talk to her about it until I'd sent it in.

"You're not helping. I can't live with a boy—"

"Man," she chimes in.

"Fine. Man. I can't live with a man, and you know that. Maybe I could ask for a new roommate," I say hopefully. "Or, just give up and come home."

"No, you can't get a new roommate, and no you aren't coming home. I know I told you to, but I think you need to do this." *Well, that's a change in attitude.* "You can do this, Fate. Remember, you're starting over. No one can see your scars unless you let them. It's time to get out into the world. Just maybe this computer thought a guy was the way to go."

"I'll try, or hide in my room the whole semester. He gave me ear plugs, so either he snores or he's a partier," I say to Clarissa, speaking quietly so he doesn't hear me gossiping about him.

"I should be concerned with you living so close to a man, but I know this is a struggle for you. Take the bull by the horns and ride it…" She pauses.

"Did you just—"

"No. Well, yes. I did say it, but I didn't mean ride him! I may still see you as a child sometimes, but you're an adult now, and that's something adults do. So, I guess you may have those experiences," she continued babbling, clearly uncomfortable with the turn of our conversation. "If you want to, I guess you could do that. Ride that bull—"

"I am not going to ride him, Clarissa!" I yell.

Knock, knock.

"Ride who, Fate?" Cameron says slyly from behind my door.

"Oh, great, thanks, Clarissa, he heard me," I say quietly into the phone.

"Oh, goodness." Clarissa chuckles in my ear. Well, that will be an awkward thing to explain. Have fun with that. You can do this, I promise."

I say my goodbyes and decide now is as good a time as any to leave my room. Especially since I heard him go out the front door. I grab my clothes and get my bathroom stuff together. Hopefully, I can get ready and be gone by the time he gets back. *He...a man.* There on the counter is a case of beer, clearly he's made himself at home. The large flat screen TV dominates the room. He has an expensive Blu-Ray collection to go with it. At least I can say he's not messy, right?

Closing my eyes, I take a deep breath. Then I open them and walk into the bathroom. I'm stunned when I run into something hard, and my eyes pop wide open as I stumble backward and almost fall on my behind. Warm, wet arms catch me before I hit the floor. I let out a groan and look up.

There he stands, holding me with a smirk on his face. I'm unable to stop my eyes from wandering. He has a large spiral tribal-type tattoo on the left side of his chest. Some words are nestled within the design, but the only one that I can read is *judge*. A small cough lets me know he's caught me staring at him.

"If you wanted to join me, you're a little late, but... I could always get back in," he says with a wicked grin on his face.

"I...oh...I mean...sorry..." I mumble.

"Fate, I'm kidding. I should have locked it. I'm just not used to having a roommate. I'll try to remember from now on," he says sincerely.

All I can do is nod. It's hard to concentrate as he still has his hands on me. It's sending my body into a panic at the closeness of someone else to me. *Breathe, Fate.*

I gulp in a couple of slow, deep breaths and try to calm myself, but it's no use. I pull myself out of his grip and turn to leave the bathroom. He grabs my wrist, and I just stare at him. I'm sure he can see in my face that I'm barely holding it together. As his grip loosens, I pull away and walk to my room. I throw everything that I took with me to the bathroom onto my desk, then I turn and lock the door. There's only one thing I can do now…crawl under the blankets and hope the world swallows me up. He probably thinks I'm a freak. If only I could deny it. I am a freak. One who can't be touched by others, among all the other issues I have. Maybe this is all too soon.

Knock, knock. "Fate, I'm going to get something to eat for dinner. Do you want to come?" His voice holds such pity. This isn't because he wants to. It is because he feels like he upset me.

"I'm just really tired. I'm going to take a nap." Shuffling at the door gets my attention. The knob begins to jiggle, and I know he's trying to open it. "Maybe another time," I say, hoping this will appease him.

"Tomorrow, after all of our classes?" My heart picks up speed because I know I'm going to have to say yes. I can't blow off my roommate.

"Screw it, world, I'm here," I quietly repeat my mom's words.

"What?"

Oh crap, he heard me.

"Yeah, that sounds good. Tomorrow then." What did I just get myself into? I hear him backing away from the door, and my body begins to relax again. At the sound of the door shutting, I sneak to peek out my bedroom door. He seems to be gone. I grab my shower things again and make my way back to the bathroom. The door is open, so at least I know I won't be having a run-in like earlier. After I lock the door, I quickly take my shower and hustle back to my room before I run into Cameron again tonight. It's still so bright out here, and the city just seems to be starting its day. I get into my pajamas again and sit on my bed with my book. My eyes grow heavy; I should have slept more today.

My eyes spring open, and I'm in a cold sweat. Someone is shaking me, and I scream even louder than I already was.

"Fate, it's me, Cameron," he says, trying to soothe me, but this only escalates my panic. It's dark in my room. I must have nodded off and slept longer than I planned. Did I forget to lock the door and turn the light on?

"Light, please," I whisper between breaths. He quickly gets up and flicks the light on. He comes right back to sit on my bed with me. He's just wearing a pair of pajama pants, leaving his whole chest bare. I finally get a chance to see his tattoo. It covers his heart and some of his shoulder. The words say *No Judgment* surrounded by the intricate design. He was sleeping. Looking over at the clock, I'm surprised to find it's after midnight. I must have been exhausted to sleep that long. "I-I'm sorry I woke you," I sputter.

"You were having a nightmare or something. I know you're not supposed to wake someone, but you just sounded so scared," he whispers to me as if afraid I'll start screaming again any minute.

"Did I say anything?" Sometimes I don't just scream, I can also talk during the episode.

His eyes bore into mine, and I'm exposed unable to keep my demons at bay. "I didn't notice anything, really. I just wanted to wake you."

Oh good, but still, I woke him. "I'm sorry, Cameron, I didn't mean to wake you. You shouldn't have to deal with this," I say more to myself than him.

"Fate, I'm not sure what this was about. I don't expect you to tell me. You just met me, but don't think everyone's life is all roses. We've all got stuff that screws with us. Life's price." His words are comforting, but my mind is somewhere else. Something he said brings me back. Back there. To my nightmare.

"Don't, please," I beg as I pull away, but it's no use. It never is.

"This is the price of the life we live," he says.

"Fate..." Cameron's voice pulls me from my memory and soothes my rapid breathing. "I lost you for a minute there."

"Sorry, I spaced out," I say, trying to brush it off. "Thank you, Cameron. I'll make sure this doesn't happen again. You didn't ask for a roommate with these issues," I add without thinking.

"Stop."

I shrink back. He moves as though to lay his hand on mine, but I quickly pull away.

"Sorry. Just don't, okay? Don't be sorry for something you're not doing on purpose. Save the 'sorry' for when it's something in your control. That's what I had to learn to do." Maybe, just maybe, this won't be as bad as I thought. He could be going to the residence committee saying I'm crazy and a problem. But he seems to understand. However, that doesn't mean I'm going to let him touch me.

"Thank you, Cameron. I won't bother you again."

He gives me a look almost as if he's saying, *really, Fate, I thought we covered this.*

"Sorry."

A smirk twists one corner of his mouth, but the look

in his eyes is the same.

"Ah. Ya. Well, this was fun. You should get some sleep," I say, hoping to get him out of here. This is my safe zone.

He gets the hint and rises. Turning to the door to leave, he stops with his hand on the doorknob and glances back at me. "Fate, we all have a fucked-up past or a screwed-up life. Don't let it define you." He gives me a small smile. "Give Fate a new definition." He grins and slowly closes the door as he leaves.

A new definition for Fate? As in me or fate itself?

Chapter Three

Fate

DAY ONE OF CLASSES seemed to go fine. No one bothered with me, which could be both good and bad. Everyone was just talking about classes and who's who. Nothing but small talk, which is, unfortunately, something I don't do well. As I walk into residency, Cameron is standing there with a group of girls around him. They all seem to be gushing, and he's enjoying the attention. *Of course he is, he's normal.* I can't stand when the attention is on me. Quickly, I make my way around them, hoping he doesn't catch me.

Maybe I can get out of dinner tonight. I'm so tired, I need to take a nap. Stealing a glance over my shoulder, I catch him watching me, ignoring the girls who are obviously trying to get him to pay attention to them. They all have plenty of skin showing. Not me. I hide as much as possible. Less chance to be touched or at least when it happens, it isn't skin to skin. Once I'm inside our apartment, I take a deep breath. I got home free without getting tagged. But then I walk over to my room and discover a note posted on my door. Peeling it carefully off, I don't even have to look at it to know that it's from Cameron.

It has a smiley face on it too. *Crap.* Well, so much for getting out of dinner and hiding out in my room alone all night. A glance at my watch informs me that I can get a few hours of sleep. Maybe he will be preoccupied with those girls downstairs and leave me alone. I get into some yoga pants and a T-shirt then climb into bed to get some rest. It will help tonight when everyone else is sleeping.

BANG, BANG.

"Rise and shine, Fate. Dinner in thirty!" Cameron yells from the other side of my door.

I groan and look at my clock. It's six-thirty on the dot. *Are you serious? I want more sleep.* I roll over and throw my face into my pillow.

"Fate, I'm not joking. You're wasting time. At seven I'm coming in there whether you're ready or not, and I will drag you out in your kitty pajamas if that's what you're wearing."

"Ah, fine, I'm up," I yell back, and he chuckles. "And I'm in yoga pants for your information," I say with as much attitude as I can muster.

"Just yoga pants? Well, that would be an interesting dinner."

Groaning, I hop out of bed and throw open the door, then shoot him an irritated glare.

He laughs again, almost bending over in a full fit of merriment. "Oh, darn, shirt too."

I raise one of my eyebrows and cross my arms.

He puts his hands up in defense. "I'm kidding, Fate. I'm sorry. I don't usually hang out with girls. I don't know how not to make jokes. Bear with me, I'm a quick learner, I promise."

"It's fine. I'm just not used to hanging out with anyone."

His smile slips, and he opens his mouth to say something, but I cut him off.

I don't want his pity. I didn't mean to say that. "My time is ticking." Then I slam my door in his face, and he bursts into a chuckle again.

"Tick-tock."

No joke, he was banging on my door at exactly seven. Luckily, I was ready, not that it takes me long to get ready. I don't wear makeup or anything to draw people's attention to me. I put on just a pair of jeans and a black, long sleeve, V-necked shirt. As I said, nothing fancy or flashy. I learned long ago not to stand out.

"I'm ready," I say as I open the door, and he's standing right there.

He really is beautiful in an obvious sort of way. I almost can't look away. All he has on is a pair of dark jeans and a blue T-shirt that hugs him in all the right ways.

I'm so out of my element here.

"Well, look at that. A girl who can get ready in a reasonable amount of time. I like it," he says in a joking way.

"Don't get used to it. I'm sure I'm not like most girls here. I won't spend hours getting ready for anyone. This is me. I'm just Fate," I say quietly.

"Yes. Yes, you are." I'm not sure what to take from what he's saying to me, so I just walk to grab my jacket. He's walking close behind me, I can tell, but he stays just out of reach so we don't accidentally touch. Cameron seems to be picking up on my issues and adapting. It's good that he's that observant, but it also embarrasses me that it's needed. "Any idea where you want to go?"

"Um, I don't know. Anywhere, really. I've only been to one little Italian place, so I'll let you pick. It was your idea," I say, trying to give a smirk at the end.

"Perfect. Time to go, Fate." He leads me out of the apartment, still careful not to touch me.

We get into a cab and find our way to a little restaurant. Nothing fancy but very secluded.

"This is one of my favorite places. They have a bit of everything. Even vegetarian food."

I shoot him a questioning gaze.

"Oh, I saw all the nature artwork and wildlife in your room and thought maybe you didn't eat meat."

I actually laugh, a full, no-holding-back laugh. "No, I eat meat. Steak, burgers, sausage…"

He gives me a grin, and I catch on to his innuendo. Playfully, I swat at him, and he chuckles as he gets out of my hand's reach. Seems I'm getting better at getting some of the social cues on interaction and all the jokes.

"I like anything, okay? I'm not picky was all I was trying to say."

"Gotcha," he says with a smirk while leading me to the back corner of this place. It's a little booth style seat just for two. With his hand, he points to either side. I just shrug my shoulders and pick the one with my back to the place. Maybe I won't be as anxious if I don't see the other people looking at us.

"So, Fate, tell me about yourself."

Here it comes, small talk. "Well, I turned eighteen three weeks ago."

His face turns to shock.

"Didn't you read your roommate sheet?" I say, trying to deflect whatever he's about to say.

"No, I figured it wouldn't matter. We'd learn about each other the old-fashioned way. But I'm assuming you did. If you didn't want a male roommate, why didn't you say something when you got your fact sheet?"

I'm stunned. Never had I thought that I was actually showing him that I didn't want a male roommate.

"Honestly, it wouldn't matter the gender of my roommate, it would still be an adjustment. I'm sorry if I gave you the impression it's you being a man or you at all that is the issue. Just an adjustment. I'm sure it will all work itself out. I'm just not the same as you, is all."

One of his eyebrows rises, and I know I've said something to warrant a response. "So you think you have me pegged? Tell me, Fate. Who am I?"

My name on his lips is laced with sarcasm, and I shrink away from the table, putting my hands in my lap.

After a moment, he breaks the silence. "I'm sorry, Fate, I didn't mean to sound that way. I just don't appreciate being judged."

"I didn't mean it offensively, I'm just observant, so I know we are different in the social aspect."

"Okay, explain." Just like that, as always when I feel I'm put on the spot, I go to what I know.

"You're like a schooling fish, you just love people and that's just not me. I can't explain it," I say to Cameron without looking in his eyes.

"So you're a beta fish then?"

I'm stunned to be having this conversation. He is actually talking to me about it and not just staring at me as a freak talking about fish. "Actually, that's probably one of the easiest ways to explain it," I say honestly.

"But those get along with the other gender, so we're good," he says with a big smirk.

"Unfortunately, that is false. They enjoy being alone no matter the gender. They also hide. Caves, rock formations... but always alone," I babble on like I just can't stop these things coming out of my mouth.

"Well, there has to be an exception or there

wouldn't be any of them since they have to mate." I go to open my mouth, but he puts his finger to my lips. I am immediately uncomfortable but less because he's touching me. It's more that I didn't flinch. "I know you could probably give a scientific answer to this, but just leave it. You can hide and be the rare, lonely Beta fish. But I'm not going to let you do it forever. No one should hide their whole life away, alone."

In that moment I feel as if this might actually work. I could have a friend. Then a girl excitedly screams. "Oh my God! It's you." Her words make me shrink back. Who does she think I am? Then I notice she is glancing at Cameron. His face is scrunched up. He looks frustrated, but he quickly turns to a cheerful smile.

"Yes, hello, and you are?" he says to the girl, who is maybe two years older than me.

"Oh, it is you. My name is Cara. I can't believe I'm standing in front of Cameron McAlister. No one will believe me. Can I take a picture with you and maybe get an autograph?" He stands, and the girl grabs on to him and turns her phone to take a picture of them both. I just sit there, trying to appear invisible. She hands him a notebook, and he puts it down on the table in front of me as he signs it, *Cameron McAlister,* and underneath it writes, *Ten Ways Gone.* He quickly hands it to her, and she gives him a hug.

"Well, Cara, enjoy your night," he says, trying to dismiss her.

"Oh, I'm sorry to interrupt your date. I didn't realize, thank you again." She looks at me with envy, and I want to correct her, but Cameron talks, silencing me.

"Thanks for understanding and letting me get back to my date." She leaves but tosses a few glances over her shoulder on her way to the door. I can't think, my mind is spinning. Who is this guy, and what the heck did I get myself into? Whatever it is, I know I just can't deal with it right now. Quickly, I grab my purse and take off out the door.

"Fate, wait. Let me explain," he calls from behind me, but I don't stop.

A cab is waiting outside and without giving it any thought, I hop in, telling the driver where to go. Just as we are taking off, Cameron comes out the door, his eyes darting back and forth, obviously seeking me. Talking to him about this right now isn't something I can do without more information. Who thinks to look up their roommate on Google before moving in? The last thing I need is to be living with someone in the spotlight. I've come too far and given up too much for it to come crashing down around me.

Chapter Four

Fate

As soon as I'm in the apartment, I rush to my room and lock the door behind me. I turn on my laptop and type the name Cameron McAlister into the search engine. Headlines pop up, and my heart drop.

Party boy leads to trashed hotel room… Musician Cameron taking time off for education… Stories leaked of backstage sexual behavior worry executives… Time to clean up the image of lead man Cameron McAlister.

My roommate is a celebrity, and not just any type. A musician.

"Hush. We don't need people to hear you."

I want to cry, but he either likes that or it makes him angrier with me. He gets up, goes to the radio, and turns it on. Music comes through, drowning out the sounds I might make. Focusing on the music is all I can do to get myself away from here.

"I should have told you."

My breath catches and my heart starts beating out of control when I look up to see Cameron standing in the doorway.

"Thought I locked that," I groan, frustrated with

myself.

"You did," he says, holding up a little screwdriver. His eyes drift to the computer screen. "But I guess now you think you know all about me."

Carefully closing my laptop, I'm torn as to what to say. "Cameron, I'm sorry I reacted that way. It's just— I'm not used to being around that or having that kind of attention given to someone with me. As I said, you're a schooling fish, happy in a crowd. Where I just want to be left—"

"Alone? Right, and you don't think that someone can be alone in a crowd. Let me tell you something. You may sit here and be alone, but don't think that with all those people I feel any less alone. If anything, it's worse to be surrounded and feel secluded. Open your damn eyes, no one is perfect. We can't all live in a perfect world like you."

As soon as he says it, I can tell he regrets it, but I can't let it go. "Perfect. Perfect? That's what you think my life is. How can you even say that to me? Did you not wake to me screaming? I can't handle the dark, okay? Does that sound like a normal, perfect life to you?" I yell at him. It feels amazing but wrong at the same time.

"We all have some loose screws. Unfortunately, no one is untainted these days, Fate. It doesn't mean that's the whole story. It's just the beginning."

I want to hear his words, but I know this isn't that world. "Maybe for a rock star who can just start his whole life over and forget about the girls he's screwed over and the rules he's broken, but I can't. I don't have money to just throw at people or the education to shut them up. I have too much to lose and far more to prove to get involved with the limelight. I. Don't. Want. This," I scream. I've never had so much emotion in a conversation.

"There you go with that judgmental shit again. Who doesn't have a history of some kind? Clearly you do, so I thought there'd be some compassion. What the hell is that saying about glass houses…?"

"People who live in them shouldn't throw stones," I yell back at him.

"Well, if you know it, stop throwing them. I don't know who fucked with you, but damn, just get under someone else. The world isn't as screwed up as you're making it out to be. People screw up, that doesn't mean they're all bad." He sneers at me, and the look in his eyes makes me take a step back.

Why are you egging him on, Fate? "Get under someone else? Yes, because that will solve everything," I say, almost choking over tears at the last part. *I will not cry.*

"Oh, the ice princess can feel things. She's not the cold-hearted person she pretends to be." His words are laced with rage.

His words enrage me. "Now who's judging?" I stick my chin out, trying to hold face. "I'm sorry I'm not like all the other girls drooling over you and your assets. Should I have just crawled in bed with you on day one? Would that have made me not a freaking ice princess?"

"Who says I would take you to my bed? Hmm, I believe that's wishful thinking on your part, darling. When I said 'date' tonight to that fan, I did it to save face. As you said, I'm a rock star. What would I want with the ice princess?"

"*Princess…*" *He says it, and I want to scream out for*

someone, but I know there isn't anyone coming. The music is on again.

"Don't. I'll tell."

"No, you won't, because no one wants you, and if you tell, they never will." His voice is cold.

"Fate." Cameron is calm and now trying to talk to me again. He takes a step forward.

"Don't. Touch. Me," I say as calmly as possible.

He moves toward me again. "Fate, please."

"I said don't," I scream, and he halts right away. "I didn't think tonight was a date because you're right, I'm ice. I don't feel anything because when I do, it's too much to bear. So please just leave me alone. You've done enough. Said enough. So just stop." He looks so sad; I'm growing exasperated with his demeanor. "Don't worry about me. Just go out and do what you do. From what I've read it's screw any girl and not care about them. Just don't bring them in here. I don't need you and your groupies trashing our apartment."

"Oh hell, you are just the same as every other girl. All about Fate," he yells back, then turns and walks out of our apartment, slamming the door closed.

What did I just do? I want to go after him, but I know it won't change anything. He's probably like me; he just needs to cool off, and we could just talk about this again tomorrow, but my mind is telling me to deal with this head on. I turn, going back to my room, but I leave my door open. We can't leave it this way.

Hours go by, and it's after midnight when I hear the students coming back and doors being shut in the hallway. They are all loud and clearly intoxicated. It's the first week, and apparently this is what some students do. But that's not me. I've never even had a drink or smoked a cigarette. Drugs, not ever going to happen. Being in my own head is bad enough without added influences. There is a slam and I peek out of my room to see if it's Cameron. It isn't. The neighbor just got in. I go back to my reading. Almost instantly, the wall behind me is banging.

It's steady and consistent, and mingled with lots of moaning from a clearly happy girl on the other side. I'm not a prude, I just…I just don't. Mumbled words join the sexual cacophony, but I try to block them out and go back to my book. The thumping and moaning only gets louder. *At least someone is having fun.* The picture hanging on the wall above my bed falls down. That's the last straw.

I pound on the wall. "Can you please move the bed away? I would like to not get killed by my pictures," I yell at the wall. For a moment, the noises dissipate, but then they are back to it again.

"Oh, yeah," filters through from the other side, and my heart stops. "Say it, baby, say my name."

"Ah… oh…" she says between moaning. "Cam…" she says and just like that, everything I felt is gone as the bricks go back up around me my heart. The noise from them picks up pace and she yells out. Then, just like that, it's done. No more sounds. They're finished. Five minutes later, he is stumbling through the door.

I walk up to my bedroom door and lean against the jamb. "What, no cuddling or sleep over?" I ask sarcastically.

"Sorry, ice princess, this ain't a fairytale," he slurs out. *Great, he's loaded.* He uses the back of the chair to hold himself up.

"Some fairytale that would be, getting it on when

she didn't even know your name. That just sounds magical. It's what I've always dreamed of." I groan.

"Cut the cute crap, Fate. It's only going to lead where you don't want to go. Or do you?" he says, raising his eyebrow.

"Is it so bad that I just want to be your friend? I don't need to screw you to prove that, do I? Didn't know that was a requirement, but I do know as a friend I didn't deserve to hear that," I say firmly.

"Why do you even care, Fate?" He walks toward me, and my hands automatically go up as a barrier between us. His chest is right against my hands. I don't flinch, I don't pull away. "Hear something you'd want to try?"

Something in me snaps. I push him as hard as I can. "Just because I wasn't trying to get you into bed after knowing you for all of five minutes doesn't mean I needed to hear that. I've never even done most of that. You didn't have to prove anything by taking our neighbor home," I say quietly.

"Next time I'll put music on so you don't hear." His words are like ice running through my veins. "Did we interrupt your sleep, princess?"

"No, you didn't. I don't sleep at night, only during the day. And no, don't put music on. That's what he did," I blurt then freeze. His words have me unable to think.

"Fate."

With a show of defiance, I meet his stare. It's like he's trying to see into me. But I know my walls are too thick, and besides I've already let him in too much as it is. "As soon as you walked out that door, I wanted to go after you, and I'm glad I didn't. You just proved you are exactly what those articles said you were. You don't want to be judged, Cameron McAlister? Then don't do those exact things. I don't need to judge you, you did that one all by yourself," I say, and then I close my door with a soft click.

Chapter Five

Cameron

WATCHING HER CLOSE THAT door on me, damn. Hard shit right there. Not that I didn't deserve that. I was an idiot. I wouldn't blame her if she never talks to me again. Where did half that crap I said even come from? Oh hell, that would be the whiskey. She just had me so riled up I had to get out of the apartment. When I got here, I expected to have some roommate who was either a guy who wanted to get in on this wingman action, or a girl trying to get me into the sack. Never did I think that someone like Fate would be the one to come walking into my life, and I royally screwed that up. Not saying I'm trying to get in her pants, but I'm not saying I'm not either. That whole night I was talking out my ass about not wanting a girl like her. She's fricking beautiful, but someone got there first. Instead of showing her every damn day how amazing she is, they destroyed her.

It's been three weeks since that night. She hasn't said anything to me other than a hello or goodbye. I've tried to get her to talk, but she just isn't having it. All the usual stuff isn't working either. Charming Cameron didn't get anywhere due to my anger being the first side she saw of me. Classes have been kicking my ass, mostly because she's in most of them. She's studying Law, and I'm Legal Studies with a Business Ethics Concentration. I wanted to go straight Law, same as her, but I'm kind of glad I didn't. I couldn't handle being with her in all my classes. Not with her shutting me out.

I haven't even touched a girl since that night. Not because I'm trying to get with Fate. Coming here, I was supposed to be getting my shit together but the first person who gave me a chance, I showed them I was that guy in the gossip articles. Usually, I don't care what people think of me. All a part of the world I live in, but this girl just saw through me and screwed it all up. I didn't even see her coming. She just showed up in my room introducing herself like it was an everyday conversation. Then, to see I was a guy, well, I'm sure that didn't make her feel better, but I wanted to get along with her. I definitely thought when she ran away she knew who I was and wanted to get dolled up. Nothing surprised me more than when she opened that door wearing those kitty pajamas. She still had no idea who I was, and I loved it.

Telling her should have been the easy part, but I didn't want her to get any preconceived ideas was about me. I hate being judged. When I met that girl at the party she was wearing a little badge that said which residence she was from, and there were a bunch of the girls from this floor. When I heard she was our neighbor, it would be awesome to say it didn't have anything to do with why I choose her, but it did. My dumbass drunk brain decided I'd show *her*. Well, I sure did. I showed Fate I was exactly what she thought of me. I've been giving her space in classes these past three weeks, but that shit is about to change.

Walking up to her, I take the seat right next to her. I waited until the last minute so she couldn't move. Okay, I trapped her, but she really didn't leave me many options. Not talking to her ever again definitely wasn't one.

"What are you doing?" she whispers at me and I can see the irritation all over her face. Giving Fate the sexiest grin I can, I just stare at her and shrug.

"Cameron, this isn't funny. I'm here to learn. This isn't helping."

"Well, if you didn't ignore me at home, I wouldn't have to go to such fricking lengths to get to you," I say quietly.

"I'm not ignoring you, I just don't have anything to say. I think we've said enough, don't you?" she asks.

Damn, she's good. "Yes, but did we say all the right things?" She gives me a confused look, and I know I'm getting somewhere. Best trick: confuse her into agreeing to what I want. "I have a lot I need to say and a whole different way to say it. Unfortunately, I don't think you'd be too pleased with those actions."

She just stares and starts to fidget. "Are you flirting with me?" she asks, and her voice is full of shock.

Shit, she's more confused, and now I'm getting confused. *Was I flirting with her?* "When I am, you will know it," I say confidently. Hopefully, that will bring some order back to this conversation. This isn't about anything other than being her friend. *Right now at least.* "I won't stop, Fate. We have a lot of classes together, and I will sit next to you in every one until you let me say what I have to say."

She huffs and her shoulders sag. Victory. "Fine, but if you're drunk or bring a groupie to the apartment tonight, I'm never even going to glance at you again, much less talk to you."

Is she jealous? God damn it. This girl screws with me in ways that should be illegal. "I swear."

She just nods in response and I let it go. She's going to talk to me. Hell, now what the hell do I say?

When class is done, she gets up and just stares at me. I didn't get a single thing out of this class. My mind was trying to figure out how to deal with our talk. "Well, let's go talk, Cameron." Quickly, I haul my ass up and grab my shit. It's go time.

As soon as we get home, she puts her stuff away and comes to sit on the couch. Instead of doing the same, I just put all my things on the table. If I go in my room, I might take a page out of Fate's book and hide.

"Let me start," she says. "I shouldn't have been so catty. You're free to do what you want, and I have no business passing judgment. You're wrong in thinking I'm perfect. I'm far from it. I'm tainted too, just as you said."

I think back to what she said about 'him turning music on too,' but I don't push. Someone made this girl into who she is. These walls and issues aren't here because of an okay life. They are here because someone completely screwed her up.

"Fate, stop. The only one who should be apologizing is me. I shouldn't have gone off on you the way I did. Calling you those names and saying everything I did was wrong. So wrong. I knew it the moment you shut that door. You said you wished you'd come after me that night. I wish you had too. I was out there knocking back drinks, telling myself to just come back and talk to you. But I was worried you'd shut me out. So, I just screwed it up more. You have your ways of dealing, so do I. If I think someone is judging me I do exactly what they expect because…hey, it's expected, so why not?"

"That's not really helping your case, McAlister," she says with a smirk. People have called me that before, but coming from Fate it just sounds sexy.

"Right. Okay, well, I'm a fuck-up. It's kind of my thing, but maybe with a little help from fate that doesn't have to be my future." She smirks and I know I'm getting some ground here.

"Now that's helping your case. Nice play on my name, McAlister." She has the sexiest and most beautiful smile when she lets it out. Not that fake shit she puts out to the world. Yeah, she is damn sexy, but right now I see the real Fate. She's so beautiful, and this girl doesn't even know it. She barely comes up to my shoulders, she's slender but not a stick. She has the figure that drives us guys crazy. Her body has curves, and I know every inch of her is perfect.

"If you keep saying my name that way, I'm going to have a really hard time being just friends," I say, hoping it comes off as a joke, but I'm dead serious. This girl has no idea of her abilities. Natural talent that is, and shit, I'm going to be pissed if it comes out with anyone else. Those ocean blue eyes should only ever look at me this way.

"Cameron," she says with this big ass grin on her face.

"Fate, that really didn't make a difference."

Her face changes, and she's either pissed or upset. *What the hell did I say?*

34

"I am not calling you Cam," she says, never glancing my way. Damn, that's what's got my girl all down. *My girl...where in the hell did that come from?* This girl has her claws in me, and she doesn't even know it. I slowly bring my hand up to her face so as not to startle her. I only have it hover over her skin, but shit, the effects of being this close to her are driving my body into overload. She flinches but only slightly. It's progress.

"I don't want you to. People who know me call me Cameron. I want you to know me. I feel as if you already do. Don't ever call me Cam," I say, trying to convey my true meaning. "Cam is what I tell girls I'm screwing around with to call me. I don't want my name tainted with that bullshit. This girl is different. I want her to see it all. The fricking flaws, the whole Cameron, definitely not just rock star Cameron McAlister. "I'm an idiot."

"I have been saying that, glad we agree," she says jokingly and pushes her hair to the side. It's some messed-up shade of red and blond, but this girl pulls it off. It's exclusive to her, it's Fate only.

"No, well, yes. Girl, you have me all twisted with my words. I meant I don't even know your last name. I know you clearly have a thing for nature, maybe fish with all those schooling fish comments, and you like quiet. You're eighteen, which was a huge shock. From class, I know you're smart as hell, but I don't even know your last name." How did that not ever come up?

"It's just a name, Cameron. I'd rather you know me than my name." She's being evasive.

"Come on, give it up, Fate," I say, grinning.

"McKenzie. Fate McKenzie," she says with a smile that reaches her eyes, and I see those walls coming down. With that it's decided, I never want to not know this girl.

"Fate McKenzie and Cameron McAlister. Sounds like fate," I say, nudging her.

"Lay off, McAlister." She pushes me jokingly.

"Fine, McKenzie, now that we've done the *I'm an asshole* talk and you forgive me, can I take you to get something to eat? My treat."

"Well, the forgiveness depends…" she trails off. She's being coy and she knows it.

"On?" I say, hoping it's something I can make happen.

"Depends how good dinner is," she says with a smirk, and I just want to keep her here to myself. Screw sharing this girl with the outside world, but I did promise dinner.

"Oh, that won't be a problem, get ready for the best damn dinner of your life, McKenzie. One order of forgiveness coming up."

Chapter Six

Fate

"THE FOOD WAS AMAZING, Clarissa. We have to go there when you come to visit. I've never tasted anything like it," I say excitedly into the phone. It really was the best thing I've ever had.

"So you forgave him?" she asks in a serious tone. I didn't tell her everything, definitely not about the neighbor. Just that he was being a jerk, but she still had her mom voice on.

"I wasn't so wonderful either, Clarissa. We both said things we didn't mean. Must have been first week frustration," I say to her, trying to downplay all this. Cameron has been the friend I've never had since I was a child. Yes, there are some feelings there on my part. He doesn't know. I haven't said anything. It isn't as if I can do anything about it. I can't even handle being touched. How would that work with someone as experienced as Cameron? Plus, he's a rock star. I don't need that kind of spotlight put on me, and the fact that he is entirely out of my league makes it impossible.

"McKenzie, it's dinner time, let's go," he yells from behind my door. "If you don't come out, I'm coming in.

You know I can get in there."

"I'll take that as you have forgiven him then?" Clarissa asks.

"Yes, I have. He's given me no reason not to. You know how I am. You have nothing to be worried about. Everything is fine." Cameron starts banging on the door like the crazy man he is. "I'm coming, Cameron. Don't go all lock picker on me."

"Last warning, Fate," he says with a few more bangs to my door.

"Lock picker," Clarissa says from the other side of the phone.

Crap, just what she needed to hear. "It's an inside joke thing. I have those now because I have friends. Be happy for me. I'm fine, I promise," I say truthfully to her.

"I'll see for myself on Thanksgiving if I don't see you before then."

Wow, was that a warning? Just then, my door bursts open and I jump.

"Time's up, say bye," he says with a serious grin on his face, but I can tell he's fighting to hide a grin.

"I have to go before I get thrown over a shoulder and carried away to dinner. Bye, Clarissa."

Reluctantly, she says goodbye, and I hang up.

"I didn't know that was an option," he says, trying to hold that serious demeanor.

"It's not," I say, and I know he knows I'm being truthful.

"Not yet. One day, Fate." I give him a long gaze, trying to show my doubt, but he just laughs it off. "I'm going to help you, and you're going to help me."

"I know what I'm going to need help with, but what

could you possibly need from me?"

"You sell yourself short, Fate. There are lots of things I can learn from you. You're my grounder."

Never have I been so confused by anyone. He says things that make me wonder if he's truly seeing the real me.

"You keep me level, which is something I need. When shit is left up to me, only God knows what the hell I'd get up into. Plus, you're not bad company," he says and, when I look at him, the smile he is giving me makes me want to shiver, but in a whole new way.

This is not what I need right now, definitely not with my roommate of all people. This can go wrong in so many ways… all leaving me completely wrecked. "Cameron," I say with such desperation. I don't know what I'm really asking him when I say his name. There is this overwhelming need to be close to him, to touch him, and I'm just not sure where that would lead.

"Fate, don't over think anything, okay? I have no agenda here. We are friends. I understand that's what you need and want." His words are like something from my own head but they are a bit off.

"What I need is you to be my friend, but what I want is something completely different." I hear his breath catch, and I quickly try to repair the damage I've done. "I know I'm not the kind of girl you go for, but you're a rock star. Can't blame a girl, can you?" I say, trying to come off as joking.

"What do you want from me, Fate? I need you to lay it out for me because sometimes I'm just not sure with you and I don't ever want to do anything to make you feel uncomfortable around me." He is putting me on the spot and the attention begins to get to me.

"Dinner," I say, trying to remind him of his early rush to get something to eat.

"You mean a date?" he says with a grin, and I know he's trying to get a read on me. It's what Cameron does. Since I have been here, I've been watching him. Even when I wasn't talking to him all that time, I couldn't help it. He just appeared so withdrawn, which seemed to be so unlike him. At night, in my room, I'd glance at pictures of him and his band. He is so at peace on stage, it's his happy place. I had to know what someone like that had to prove by behaving the way he was to me. I couldn't shake him off.

"I don't know how to date. I've never even had a friend. I don't let people in or let them even touch me. It's the way I've survived." I can see my words are hurting him, but they need to be said. "I can't make any promises. Each step is a new one and they all have to be small." He is hopeful and that brings me the feelings I was wanting. "But I'm willing to try."

"I'm going to be the good guy. I don't want you to think my intentions aren't pure here. So I will be your friend." His words make my heart sink. I try to keep my face straight and I know I'm failing miserably. "It's not because I don't want more. Trust me, that's the farthest from the truth here, but I won't rush this and risk screwing it up again."

I could just lean over and touch him, but just the thought of contact is driving my heart into overdrive. "You challenge me, McAlister, I like that about you. Don't back off too much, okay?" My mind is spiraling at my outburst. Never had I wanted to be brought out of my shell until Cameron. It's now or never! "*Sometimes you have to push through the pain*, right?" His eyes light up, and I know he's trying to figure out if that was just a coincidence. *"Only then will you see the truth behind it."*

"Fate…I know you don't enjoy music. How?" he whispers to me.

"I printed out all the lyrics. I read them, I didn't listen. I'm just not there yet. I don't know if I will get there. So I'm just not sure how this will work but… *I'm willing to leave it all behind for a chance."*

"Stop, please." He grimaces as if he's in so much pain, and I worry that this may be a trigger for him similar to how touching is for me.

"I'm sorry, I thought you'd be happy. I never meant to bring up anything that would give you such pain, Cameron." I walk away and sit on the couch, putting my hands in my lap. Within a few seconds, he's sitting next to me. His hand goes to touch my leg, but he stops himself.

"Fate, it isn't a bad memory. You have no idea what it means that you put yourself through that shit to read my words. Then to hear you say them to me, and not just reading them, but using them as a direction for your life… well, that just breaks me. I will never push, but I want to comfort you and I just don't know how."

"You want to touch me?"

"Fate," he says, and I know he's feeling my struggle.

"Close your eyes, Cameron." He shakes his head and tries to get up. I do the first thing I think of and place my hand on his leg to stop him. It does and he glances up into my eyes. I move my hand away and give him a small smile. "Close your eyes."

He does what I ask and his breathing labors. Slowly, I bring my hand up and lightly place my hand against his cheek. His eyes pop open and he glances at me frantically to see if I'm handling this. "Cameron." Bringing my thumb down, I trace his bottom lip, and he shivers beneath my touch. Never have I been this bold, but something in him brings this out in me. My hand rests against his check again and I slide my fingers against his soft skin. The warmth I'm feeling off him is nothing I've felt before. It's addicting. He brings his hand to overlap mine, but he stops. "Cameron, please." He starts to put his hand down. "No, please...I want you to." His eyes are staring into mine as if he's checking for any hesitation.

"Say it. Fate." My heart begins pounding out of control as his words reach my ears.

"Touch me," I whisper. "Please." I watch as he slowly brings his hand up and covers mine with his. There I am, waiting for it, but it doesn't happen... I don't flinch. I don't sense this overwhelming pain as if I'm going to break, I just have him. That's all I need at this moment. *"Nothing feels as good as being close to you."*

"Damn it, I didn't even know what that meant when I wrote it, not until now." His words add further warmth to my body, and I know this is progress. The smile that comes across my face as he caresses my hand with his feels amazing. Light, free from the pain. A moment that is my own. Our own, one that no one can take from us. "Baby steps."

"Baby steps," I repeat.

"I won't give up on you, we are in this together." He glances at me and the connection clicks. Many years from now, I can say this was that moment I started to shed my walls and become Fate again. "I never meant these when I wrote them, but hell I do now." My breath halts and I try to focus on the touch of him. *"One life is what I choose, and I choose it with you."* When I read those lyrics, I felt drawn, but having him read them to me is something I could have never imagined.

Chapter Seven

Fate

"WE ARE GOING TO have to order in," Cameron says, and a sudden rush of happiness happens. That means more time with just Cameron, and I don't mind that at all. "Unless, do you need to go sleep?" His words remind me that I haven't napped today and I will be extremely tired tomorrow. I just can't bring myself to give up any time with him right now. "I know you don't sleep at night. I won't ask you why, but you are not the only one who watches people. I noticed a pattern and I want to work around those things so I don't become a problem."

"You are not a problem. I would tell you if you were."

He glances at me, and I can tell he's struggling with how to approach something. "That's the only way this is going to work. I need to know when to stop. Some way to know you're struggling, so I can be sure I'm not adding to it. A code word or something to let me know I have to stop right away. So pick one." He is putting me on the spot, and I begin to feel uncomfortable.

"Okay, if picking the code word makes me feel uncomfortable, how is this supposed to work?" I sigh and look at my hands.

"Damn, let's see. It's not the idea of the word, right? It's having to come up with one yourself." Glancing up at him, I give him a slight nod. "Got it, you don't like being put on the spot. I'll have to remember that. So I will pick one. Does that work better for you?" I give him a smile, letting him know that is exactly what I need. "Shit, now I have to come up with something. You're right, this on the spot crap doesn't work for anyone." He makes me laugh. It is quickly becoming one of my favorite things about him. "Choose."

"What? No, you said you would," I beg.

"No, the code word is 'choose.' That way it's easy enough to say in any situation, but only we know what it truly means." Giving him my best *I'm lost* shrug, I hope he will enlighten me on this as I'm out of the loop. *"One life is what I choose, and I choose it with you."*

Quickly, I place my hand on his, which is currently situated on his lap. At first, he flinches and I worry that it wasn't wanted, so I pull my hand away. "No," he says, grabbing my hand and then letting go as he gasps. "I'm sorry, it was a pure instinct. I didn't even think about it." My hand find's it's place back on his.

"This is all baby steps, remember? For both of us. I don't expect you to remember everything and not slip up." Slipping my thumb under his hand so we are connected, I continue, "This, your hand on my hand, I'm fine with. I can't promise I won't flinch if caught off guard, but I'm trying, and I hope you will too. *Push through the pain*, right?"

He brings his other hand to overlap mine; I wait for the warmth of his touch. It's as if my body is craving it. I want more, but I know it's too soon. If I move forward more than I'm ready, I could destroy all this progress.

"Push through the pain," he says, and I smile.

"Tell me something I couldn't find on the internet about you."

Cameron's face breaks out into a grin. "Was someone researching me while she wasn't talking to me?"

Oh crap, busted. "Well, I couldn't get the information any other way. Honestly, there isn't much about anything else except your music and the reasons you need to clean up your image. I just want to know something others don't. The whole world could know as much about you as me."

"Fate, they see a personality. A rock star, not Cameron. Just a name, that's all I am." His words remind me of the difficulties I could encounter being around him.

"Do we have to tell people?" I ask shyly.

"Tell people what?" he says coyly with a giant smirk on his face.

"About us, our friendship?"

"Is it just a friendship?"

No, it's not, but I just don't know how to say it. This moment, this exact moment in time was the day I was afraid of. The day someone wanted more from me. How can you give someone more when all that you have to give has been taken from you?

"I don't think this will ever be just friendship. I think it's always going to be more. Are you okay with that?" He appears nervous as the words escape him. He's vulnerable and my heart calls to him even though I'm shaking. Afraid of the world I'm about to enter into. He and I, a world I'd never dreamed of. Two souls, so different but yet we are the same; people that have been broken by this cruel world.

"I do like the sound of it, I just worry about the public piece. They will expect me to be this rock star groupie girl, and I don't think I can play that part." Hoping he understands me is all I can think about.

"We don't have to tell people, not yet, but it will come out one way or another. These things always do, but when it does, it will not be this crazy frenzy with it. I won't let the spotlight hurt you. Fate, I never want you to play anything. I don't want you to have to act the way you think you should. I just want you, screwed up and all, because that's what you're going to get with me… every flaw and weakness. But I trust you to help me and want to be around me anyways." His words make me feel raw and, by the looks of it, he is too. Slowly, I lower my head and put it on his shoulder. It feels nice to be comforted in such a way I'm not used to.

"Screw it, world, I'm here," I say, thinking of my mom and all the happiness she gave me.

"I've heard you say that before, never loud enough that I could be sure you were talking to me, but I have to ask. Where is that from?" His fingers caressing my hand and it only furthers my need to be close to him. It's not sexual, but comforting, a need to feel safe. One that has never been met since the day I lost my mother.

"My mother said it. She died when I was nine. She was my best friend, and I miss her every day." His hand stills and I'm waiting for it. The pity, the reason I hate talking about my life.

"My mom's dead too. It blows, doesn't it?" I can't help but chuckle. Only Cameron would be able to make me laugh at a time like this. His personality and charm have a way of making me feel as if I'm not so screwed-up.

"That sounds about right."

"Fate, you don't swear, do you?" he says in a serious tone. All I do is shake my head. "Does it bother you that I do? I never thought to ask because it's just something I do. To me it's just a word, but if it bothers you, I'll try to put a cap on it."

"It's not that I don't swear, I just haven't found a reason to. Besides, Clarissa would have been upset if I had. She was my worker at one time and she is a mom to me now, so I just never started. Kind of hard to get a vocabulary of swearing when your only friend is someone you think of as a mother."

"Worker?" he asks, and I know this is a line of questioning I hate to answer.

"She works in Child Welfare. After my mom was gone, I went into the system. She eventually got me out and took me in. I wouldn't be where I am without Clarissa."

"What about your dad?" he asks, and I still.

"He wasn't up to the job, so Clarissa stepped in. I haven't seen him in a long time. He could be dead for all I know." I hope that's enough. It's mostly the truth. I haven't seen him since a few months after my mom died and Clarissa did step in, but if he were dead she would've told me.

"My dad is gone, left when my mom told him she was pregnant. Men are assholes." He chuckles, and I can't help but laugh with him.

"You said it," I say to him, and he bumps me with his shoulder playfully. It's nice to have someone to talk with and joke with because I've never had that. I'm socially stunted, but it seems I'm finally coming along. "Do you have siblings?" He shakes his head. "Your mom couldn't handle you, I guess. Why have another Cameron to turn the world to chaos?" I say playfully.

"Hey, I didn't hear you mention sibling, so I guess that could be said about you too, you little shit," he says, and I stick out my tongue in response. "Thought so."

Putting my head back on his shoulder, I lean back into him, thinking about all the ways this could play out. How will Clarissa react when I tell her about my feelings for Cameron? How will he react when he knows how hard I'm already falling for his bad-boy charm and the beauty that is within him? He's a tortured soul, destroyed, same as me. Maybe together we can build each other back up.

"I don't know what I did to get such an amazing roommate," I say, because even without my feelings for him, he is still understanding of my limitations and a thoughtful friend.

"Fate."

"Yea?" I ask him.

"No, it was fate. That's the only way this is coming together for us. My own little piece of fate with a name to match." His words warm my heart. "I want to try something. Can you try to trust me?" Cameron says without taking his eyes off mine. "Baby steps, I promise. If it's too much, I won't try again." All I can do is nod. "Could you close your eyes?"

"I can't…" I say in a panic, my eyes now glued to the floor.

"Hey…hey, don't hide from me." Automatically, I find myself searching for his eyes. "Don't let stuff like that worry you. If you can't do it, we don't do it. Together we find a way to work through it or we don't do it. It's as easy as that, okay?" I nod. "Are you ready?"

"Ready as I will ever be." It's as if it all happens in slow motion. I bring my hand up and I wait for the panic to set in. Slowly, he lowers his lips to the top of my hand, closes his eyes and softly kisses my hand. The heat from his lips touching my skin makes my body want to squirm, but in a whole new way.

I don't panic; the only thing I feel is our connection growing, and every part of me can't wait to see what our next baby steps are.

Chapter Eight

Cameron

"So, who is she?"

"Sorry, what?" I say to Scott and try to figure out where I got lost in this conversation. I know we were talking about some new music I was working on, but then I got lost in thought. Scott was working the beats for the song, and my mind just wandered off to where it has been going a lot lately. *Fate.* "You were talking about your drums?" He shakes his head and chuckles. "Cecilia?" Hopefully, he was talking about his girlfriend.

"Man, who the hell is she? What girl has you so wrapped up that you aren't out with ladies and I'm not having to clean up your messes? Whoever she is, I need to thank her. I'm actually getting done."

"Fate."

"What's fate?" Scott questions.

"That's her name, smartass. Fate is everything a man wants, and she's damn near perfect too," I say with a goofy ass smile on my face. Lately, I have been unable to keep this lovesick puppy feeling from shining through. It's a neon sign above me pointing it out.

"So what's got your head in the clouds? Need to rush off and put your head in something else?" Scott says and I slam my hands against the table, startling him. "What the hell, man?"

"Do not go there, I'm warning you. This isn't about getting a piece of ass. I haven't even kissed her unless you count her hand."

"You don't have to kiss her to get some, you taught me that," he says with a wink, and I want to drop him right here with everyone watching. Instead of beating the hell out of my best friend, I just shake my head and throw him a warning glare. "Wow, all right then. So this is serious for you. So tell me about Fate. I have to hear how near perfect she really is, and she must be to have you this riled up."

"That's just it. She is perfect to me in every way, but unfortunately she is destroyed in so many other ways." Scott just glances at me as if he's not getting what I'm trying to say. "She's beautiful and she doesn't even know that. She just thinks she is invisible to the world and, let me tell you, she isn't. But the rest of the female population has been since she ripped me a new one for screwing the neighbor."

"You screwed the damn neighbor and she caught you? Well, she must be an angel to keep talking to you." Scott never lets things slide, not if he thinks it's just me being stupid. Which, until meeting Fate, was a lot. He was always cleaning up my image.

"Ya. Well, they share a wall, and she heard me banging the girl's headboard off the wall. Then she got all sassy and banged on the wall, yelling at us. I was completely loaded and I made the girl say my name. That way she knew it was me on the other side."

"You did not do that." He's shocked, and I've done some pretty awful things in the past. "What the hell were you thinking? This is your roommate. You can't swap her out, and you tried to piss her off the first night. Why would you do that?"

"I was thinking I didn't appreciate that she looked me up on Google then assumed I was everything she read. You know how I handle being judged." This isn't a new thing for me. When people prejudge me I either find a way to prove them wrong or, in Fate's case, do exactly what is expected. Never has that backfired on me and been thrown in my face before. "Then I walked in drunk out of my mind and she handed me my ass. It was the best and worst thing ever. She didn't talk to me for weeks." Scott just gives me a smile as if he's saying, 'and you blame her?' "I finally got her to talk to me and cleared the air. We seem to be hitting it off, but I just never know with this girl, she always has me guessing. Someone messed with her, Scott. Someone ripped her up, and I'm not sure how to put her back together again."

"Man, if she's that damaged, why are you going there? Move on, be friends since you have to live with her, but just move on," Scott says, and I just know I'm past that being an option.

"No one can beat this girl. I'm telling you, as shattered as she is, there isn't anyone else that could make me take my eyes off her," I say truthfully, not caring what kind of loser this makes me sound like to him.

Something catches his eye and he gives me this grin. "I don't know, man, look at that girl there," he says, pointing to the crowd walking by. When they clear all that's left is one girl reading in the lounge. "She's better than damn near perfect."

I smile at her and she smiles back, giving me a small shy wave. "That's Fate," I say proudly, and Scott's mouth drops open.

"You're screwing with me," he says while he examines me for any of the signs that I'm lying.

"I wish I were. That's her, and now you see why I'm screwed." He just keeps staring at her and something changes in me. I've never felt this way before. I'm jealous.

"Oh, you are so screwed. That girl is going to chew you up and spit you out for fun, but I'd risk it for a chance with that," he says plainly.

"If you keep checking out my girl, I'm going to tell Cecilia and I won't have to worry about you trying to get my girl because there won't be any of you left after Cecilia is done with you." Scott shakes his head as if he's trying to clear it. *That asshole better not be thinking about Fate.*

"Okay, I'm done. Don't tell Cecilia," Scott says jokingly. He might be talking a big game, but he loves her more than life itself. He'd do anything for her and he'd never screw that up.

"Don't tell Cecilia what?" We are both startled and there is Cecilia, staring at us. She knows she's just caught us with our hands in the cookie jar.

"That someone has taken Cameron's man card, and he doesn't even want it back," he says to her as she takes a seat with us. Cecilia and Scott have been together since they were fifteen. They are that couple that everyone hates because they make their relationships out to be like dog shit in comparison.

"This, I have to hear," she says enthusiastically, and Scott fills her in on everything I told him. "So what is it that broke this girl?" she asks, and I'm not sure what to say. Not because I don't know. I have some ideas, but I'm not sure I want to share that part of Fate. I want her to trust me.

"I think someone hurt her. I'm not sure how, though. She can't be touched, so if you guys come around don't try to. It's really bad, and she can't handle it." Scott is stunned, but Cecilia just nods. "I'm going to help her."

"Well, just don't go falling for her," Scott states while Cecilia just keeps glancing between Fate and me as we keep going back and forth, catching each other staring.

"I think that advice might be a little too late, Scott," Cecilia says, and that catches my attention.

"What are you talking about, Cecilia?" Could I already be falling for Fate? "I just met her."

"That doesn't matter and you know it. Sometimes there are just people who get right in under your skin from day one or like that one pebble that stands out in the river. You just know it's for you."

"Pebbles and rivers. Well, if you talk that way around her, she will have lots to talk about," I say plainly, and she gives me a perplexed look. "She has a thing for nature. Not like hippie shit, but she's into wildlife. Fish and marine animals particularly it would seem."

"Well, she loves animals, maybe that's why she can't stop staring at you," she says, and my eyes quickly dart to Fate's. Cecilia was right, she is watching me. When she notices I caught her, she glances down at her book. She's blushing as she discreetly pulls her hair down to try to cover the evidence.

"Damn, you're right, Cecilia," I say as I realize that I'm overjoyed I'm having that effect on Fate. I'm already falling for this girl and I don't even know her secrets. I don't give a shit what they are either. From everything I'm already feeling, I know that this isn't just some girl to me. "How did that happen?"

"Sometimes, you have no control over things. Someone will come into your life and you lose yourself." I stare at her because I'm confused by whatever the hell she's trying to say. "You have no control because that 'right' someone comes in and they take it all. That 'right' girl for you might just be Fate."

Glancing back at Fate, she gazes at me again and she quickly diverts her eyes again. *Damn, she's right. That girl is Fate.*

"He is just needing to get laid. He hasn't got any since Fate caught him banging the neighbor. He almost put the chick through the wall just to prove he wasn't a big man whore like the media says he is," Scott replies, and Cecilia gives me a disapproving smile.

"Are you stupid? Seriously, sometimes you only think with your dick, Cameron. You better not do that with this girl or you are going to lose her, and I'm sure someone else will gladly take your place," she says with a smirk, and I scowl at her. "Don't be a dumbass. Men notice her even though she's trying to blend in. That girl was born to stand out, and if you mess this up, there will be a line of men to take your spot." I notice Cecilia is right. The guys are watching her, and she doesn't even notice that some are trying to get her attention. Cecilia stands up and grabs her bag.

"Where are you going?" I ask her.

"I'm going to meet Fate, because clearly she needs a friend who she can talk to about all the shit you put her through." With that, she takes off in Fate's direction and all I can do is sit and watch.

Chapter Nine

Fate

HE'S LIKE NO ONE I have ever seen before. I can't stop watching him from across the room. When he caught me a moment ago staring at him, I felt my whole face go red. I almost got up and went back to the apartment. To be honest, the only reason I stayed was because I didn't want to give up the view. If he was in the apartment, that's where I'd be right now because I enjoy watching him more than anything. He's a mystery to me, and I'm drawn to him in a way I never have before.

Taking a quick glance up again, I notice the girl who was sitting there get up and make her way toward me. *Crap.* He probably has a girlfriend, and I've just pissed her off with my unwanted interest in him. When she approaches me, I wait for it, but she just stands there. "Well, come on, I don't want to stand here all day," she says to me and I'm lost. What am I supposed to be doing?

"I'm not sure I know what you mean," I reply.

"Pack your stuff, you're coming to sit with us." Her words shock me.

"Shouldn't you be running me off, or is this one of those keep your enemies close things?" I say to her, and she just laughs.

"I get what he likes about you, but I'm still not quite sure what the hell you are talking about." She is striking. No wonder she's not worried about me, I'm nowhere near competition to this girl. Her hair is a chocolate brown and curly, cascading all around her, framing her face nicely. She has matching brown eyes that pop out, and her body is one most people have to work very hard for. Everything about her is perfect.

"I'm sorry if it bothers you that your boyfriend has a female roommate. I didn't know he had a girlfriend, but I do now and I can assure you I will not interfere," I say, trying to show her I'm just being friendly. Maybe we can all be friends, even though I think it would break me to watch him be with another girl.

"He banged the neighbor so loudly that you had to yell at them to shut the hell up. Trust me, we are not together. I'm with the band's drummer, Scott. He's the one sitting next to him. But I know all about you. Let me tell you, if anyone can play the 'I'm his girlfriend' card, that would appear to be you from the way he keeps watching you." My mouth falls open at her candor. "He's a fuck-up, but we keep him anyway. So get your shit, girly, you're coming to sit with us and you might as well get used to it."

Quickly, I gather my things up because, honestly, I'm worried if I don't this girl will just drag me over there. Once I'm done, she nods toward the table, and I walk over there with her. Cameron is watching me the entire time, and I can't seem to pull my gaze from his. When I get up to the table, Cameron pulls out the chair beside him and motions for me to take the seat next to him.

"Oh, and I'm Cecilia. We're friends now and, yes, you can call me anytime to tell me he's a jackass."

Scott just laughs and leans over, giving Cecilia a kiss as she sits down next to him. Scott has jet-black hair and these crystal green eyes. He's not as lean as Cameron, but he's definitely not bad to stare at. He and Cecilia match in every level of beauty.

I glance sideways, catching Cameron's eyes again as if he is constantly watching me. Smiling at him, I can't help the happiness he has been bringing me.

"Hey," he says to me, and I can't help the warmth that floods my cheeks.

"Hey," I reply, and he just gives me that smirk I've started to enjoy.

"Awe, they just did that cute, awkward 'hey' thing," Scott says and then his face scrunches up in pain as the sound of him getting kicked under the table by Cameron echo's while Cecilia elbows him in the chest at the same time. "You both suck, and that hurt like hell. Fine, I will try something else. I've heard a lot about you but not everything I want to know. How old are you, Fate?" he says, and I'm not sure exactly what to say.

"Eighteen," I answer, and Scott spits out his coffee everywhere. "I turned eighteen right before school started," I blurt out.

Scott is a bit pale. A glance over at Cameron shows he's just watching this with amusement.

"Robbing the cradle much, man?" Scott says, and I have to gaze away from them. It never crossed my mind that age may be an issue.

"No, I just know what I like," Cameron says, and I stare up. He gives Scott a disapproving stare that mirrors Cecilia's.

Cecilia diverts the conversation and begins talking about how they all know each other. Scott and Cameron started off as childhood friends. Cecilia moved to their school at fifteen, and Scott just couldn't resist her. They both have been in school since they graduated, but Cameron was too busy with the music world and being the face of Ten Ways Gone.

"I didn't tell her who I was. That's one of the other reasons she didn't talk to me. She didn't know who Ten Ways Gone was and it was awesome," Cameron whispers.

"Well, did you grow up under a rock or not read? He's been in the tabloids for all the shit I've had to get him out of," Scott says. "Oh, thank you, by the way. You've made my life pretty easy since school started. He's staying out of trouble, so keep it up, Fate," Scott says with an appreciative smile.

"I'm from Florida, so no, not under a rock, and I read all the time, just not about who's who and all that nonsense. As for music, I don't really listen to it. You could be a Rolling Stone and I wouldn't really know. However, once I met Cameron I did look up all your lyrics, which, by the way, are incredible," I say with such admiration. "They aren't all about raising hell or what a beautiful thing love is. They are about life. I like that."

"Well, that would be all Cameron. I help with the beats, but all those words come from this little shit eater, if you can believe that," Scott says, and I'm a little stunned. Reading about the band I did see that it comes from the lead man, but that's not an unusual thing to say to bring the music to a new level with the fans. It builds the persona of that individual. Cameron squirms under my gaze and I wonder why he appears so nervous.

"Well, I should get back to the apartment. Fate, do you want to walk back with me?" Cameron asks, and I nod in response. Sitting here with his friends, without him, makes me very uncomfortable. "You might as well give Cecilia your number, or she is just going to hound me until I give it to her. Or she will show up raising hell at home," he says, and I have to admit when he says home it makes me ecstatic that this man's home is where I live too.

"He's right, so you might as well fork it over, Fate," Cecilia says, giving me a wink. Quickly, I write it down and hand it to her. This girl is opposite of me. She seems to be able to pull things from me similar to Cameron. That's a scary thought. Cameron points to the door, and I nod as we walk off together out of the building.

Once we arrive at the apartment, there is silence between us. I can sense that Cameron wants to say something, and I've never really seen him this unsure of himself. "Cameron, what's wrong?" I ask, worried I've done something wrong. "I'm sorry if I embarrassed you in front of your friends. When Cecilia came over she didn't really give me a chance to say no."

"She has that effect on people. You didn't embarrass me. Don't worry, that could never happen. I was worried they'd say something to scare you off and you'd shut me out again," he says with such honesty it seems as if I can see inside this man. He's no longer a rock star but just a man.

"I have pretty much stalked you online, there isn't much I don't know. We all have a history. No judgment, remember…" I say as I walk to the couch and sit. Cameron follows me over and lowers himself beside me.

"You're exhausted. Beautiful, but tired. How is the sleeping working out for you?" he says, and there is an urge to be brutally honest with him.

"It's not going well at all. When I was back home I was homeschooled so I could work around my issues, but here I'm finding it difficult to get into a routine." He glances at me with such sadness that my inner walls begin to shake and come down. Mentally, I reinforce them because if they come down, I don't know if I'll be able to put them back up. "Don't worry, I'm beginning to figure it all out. I might try to work my schedule differently when I pick my next set of classes."

Cameron is staring into the wall like it's going to do something crazy. "I was wondering if maybe you'd be willing to let me try to help you." I give him a confused gaze, asking him what he means, and he continues, "Well, your room seems to be an issue for you at night. So what if you keep the lights on and sleep in your bed at night?"

Shaking my head, I tell him the facts of my condition. "It's my bed too, not just the dark," I say plainly, hoping he won't ask for the reasons behind my issues.

"Do you trust me?" he asks, and I hesitate.

Do I trust Cameron? He hasn't given me a reason to not trust him. Continuously he has worked with my limitations and never tries to push me into something I can't handle. Nodding, I give him a tiny smile.

He gets up and goes to his bedroom, coming out with a pillow and a blanket. I give him a questioning glare as he goes around our common area, turning on every lamp. Instead of being closed off, I peek outside, I can see that the darkness of night has taken over the skies. "These are for you," he says as he hands me his blanket and pillow. "Since the dark and your bed are issues, let's take them both off the table. The couch won't be as comfortable, but it's all about baby steps," he says with a grin, and my smile grows. "The lights will stay on all night. I'll leave my door open, and if you need me, you can just call out to me."

"I'm not sure that I won't have nightmares or scream. I've never tried anything like this before," I say truthfully, showing him my real weaknesses.

"Baby steps," he repeats. "If you do have a nightmare, I'll be right here to wake you up, and if it becomes too much, we try another route. Go get some pajamas on."

Doing as he asks, I walk away, closing my door behind me. Once I'm dressed in my comfy kitty pajamas, I head out. There is a sheet on top of the couch and a pillow is set out for me. He is still holding the blanket, and I lie down on the couch as he watches me. "You and your damn kitties," he says with a wink, and I can't help the giggle that escapes me. Cameron places the blanket over me and tucks me in then bends down and lightly kisses my hand the same way he did before. "Goodnight, Fate," he says, and I want nothing more than for him to stay with me, but I have to try this alone.

Chapter Ten

Cameron

"Don't, please."

Waking, Fate cries out, and I jump out of bed and race to the living room. I never thought that night with her in her bed screaming could be trumped, but man was I wrong. She is twisting and struggling, still asleep. She seems so damn distressed, this unbearable need to hold her comes over me. I did this. She trusted me and I blew it. Bending down, I slowly bring my hand to hers and give it a small squeeze. "Fate," I say, and her eyes pop open. The fear is still very present in those broken blue eyes that have taken hold of me.

"Cameron," she whispers, and the sting of her pain is aching in me. *Shit.* I want to reach out to her, but I know it has to be her way. "Please," she murmurs, and I'm not sure what she is asking me for.

"What, Fate? What do you need? Anything, it's yours." Damn it, this girl is in pain because I thought I could get her past this piece of her past.

"You," she says as if at any moment she's going to be shattered to pieces. I watch as she reaches out and grabs my hand. I squeeze her gently, letting her know

I'm here for her in the only way I can.

"You never have to ask me for that. I'm sorry I pushed you to do this."

Her eyes are filled with sorrow, and I want to beat the hell out of myself for putting her through this. "It's all about finding different ways. Maybe we could try something, I'm not sure if it will work, though." She sounds so unsure I almost want to tell her to not even think about it, but at the same time I want to do anything to get her through this pain.

"What is it?" I ask, and her eyes go to my bare chest before finding my eyes again.

"Maybe you could sit with me, but..." She takes a deep breath, and it's like I'm not even taking any at all. "First, I need you to put a shirt on," she says, and I can see a smirk trying to break free from her. I let go of her hand, I go grab a shirt quickly putting in on.

"Now what?" I say, gazing at her with uncertainty. She sits up and moves her pillow, then pats her hand on the couch. Following her direction, I sit on the couch next to her. Slowly, she puts the pillow down over my lap and begins to lie down on it. Her hands come to mine and brings them down to her. Holding them, she places them next to her face and just continues to squeeze them tightly within her grasp.

"You don't have to stay this way if you don't want to," she says shyly.

"Fate, you really have no idea how much it means when you let me in, do you?" Her eyes bore into mine, baring me before her.

"You don't have to stay like this long, I just feel calm when I'm around you. I don't want you to lose sleep." Finally, she clues into the fact that it's night and we have classes tomorrow. She goes to get up, but I hold our hands firmly so she can't.

"I'm comfortable just like this. You talk as if you're the only one who feels things when we are touching. Trust me, I'm right there with you." Her mouth pops open in an *oh* expression, and I'm finally realizing that someone has truly screwed with her. She doesn't understand what a damn amazing person she is. The peace she brings me when I'm touching her. "You're not the only one with demons, Fate."

Her head rests back down on the pillow that is situated on my lap and her body let out a sigh. If my girl wasn't so damn broken, I'd wrap myself around her and protect her from anything that tries to harm her. "I'd take it away if I could," I slip out, and she tenses.

"What happened to you, Cameron? What demons do you have?"

I don't want to say anything, but if I ever want this girl to let me know hers I've got to make the first move. "It was before my mom died. My dad had passed away when I was just a baby and that broke my mom apart. She was dating this guy when I was almost sixteen who started getting rough with her." Her breath is labored and I want to stop. She doesn't need my baggage. Her eyes tell me to continue, and I can't refuse her. "I walked in on it and I lost it, Fate. All I saw was red and I beat that asshole within an inch of his pathetic life. When I threw him out, I told him if he ever came back I'd finish what I started. He never came back. Good thing he didn't because I wasn't bluffing and that's the scariest part."

"Cameron, you did what anyone would have. He

was hurting your mother, that doesn't make you a bad person." Her sweet words give me comfort that I haven't felt in years. "What happened to your mom, Cameron? Mine passed away in a car accident," she states, and those walls of hers are starting to form windows.

"This is what makes me the bad person, Fate. I don't think I can tell you." The guilt is still there.

"Cameron, my mom was on the way to get me from school. She was late and I had given her a hard time the last time she was late because I didn't like having to wait in front of the office. She was supposed to be taking me to the aquarium, she had promised. My mother was in a hurry so that I could get there and have a few hours before they closed. It was all for me and my stupid fish obsession."

This is the most she's let me in since the day I met her. I don't think she has a clue how much it means to hear her telling me about her life, even though I know she thinks this makes her weak. She's never said it, but I know showing emotions is something she doesn't do. Not because she doesn't feel them, but because someone made her think that it was a weakness.

"After my mom realized he wasn't coming back, she hated me. She got into drugs and I couldn't deal. Instead of helping her, I left and went to live with Scott's family. They knew about my mom's struggles and took me in with no questions asked. Five weeks later, my mom overdosed, and it wasn't until the mail started piling up that anyone thought to check on her. I buried her a few days before I turned sixteen. I didn't even let Scott or his parents come with me. I did it alone."

Fate's hand rests against my chest and her touch

soothes me from the memories threatening to break free. "You were just a child. You aren't expected to handle those types of things. Your mom was sick and you couldn't help her. You did what you had to. You got out, who knows what could have happened to you if you had stayed. Drugs or more violence that you couldn't walk away from... no, I can't even." She takes a pause. "That's something I just don't want to think about. You have to let it go."

"Fate, I won't make you tell me. You will when you're ready, or you may never and that's okay too. But you were just a child too. So let's both take your advice." She peers away from me for a moment, and I worry that she's putting those walls back up around her beautiful self.

"It was after my mom died. Someone hurt me, in more ways than one. They made me feel used and alone. Touching, the dark, music...it was all ruined for me. I'm just starting to get small pieces of that back, thanks to you." Her words warm me and she goes to sit up. I let her this time. After I turn around, she places both her hands on my chest, and I freeze under her gaze. "Close your eyes," she says softly, and I immediately comply.

Her hands grip my shirt and I'm stunned when her lips softly press against mine. She lingers there for a moment, then pulls away and I open my eyes. My fingers find my lips, touching them like I can't believe she just did that. A single tear trickles down her face. My happiness turns south at the sight of her. "You didn't have to do that."

"I'm sorry, I didn't even stop to think if you wanted me to. How stupid of me," she states as she pulls away from me.

Without thinking, I wrap my hands around her wrists, holding her in place before she can put any more distance between us. "I meant you didn't have to do that for me. To help my pain, it only added to yours and that's even more painful to me than all this shit."

Her eyes open wide at my confession. "I didn't do it just for your pain. I did it for mine. That was my baby step," she says as she comes to me again, placing her hands on my chest as she leans in this time, putting her lips firmly against mine. She breaks away, and there are a few tears falling this time. "I did it. We did it," she says with a smile on her face, and in that moment, I realize that these are happy tears.

"Yes, we did, my beautiful girl."

She cuddles tightly against my side, peeking up at me from where her head is lying on my chest. "My girl, I like the sound of that," she admits.

"Well, I will always be here for those baby steps. Happy tears only," I say as I bring my thumb to her cheek, wiping away the tears that remain. She doesn't recoil from me; my heart skips and I know it now. I'm completely screwed. This girl has got me right where she needs me, but better yet, right where I want to be.

"We are such a mess," she says, and I can't help but give her a smile.

The only way this appears to me is that we've had shit handed to us that we couldn't help. Together, I'm hoping we will be exactly what the other needs. "We are *beautifully destroyed*."

Chapter Eleven

Fate

I PANIC WHEN I awake, as I'm not sure where I am at first. Someone is holding me, and I can't help the tremble that comes over me. His grip tightens and he sighs. Cameron is slouched over and has me in his arms. My fear disappears at the realization it is him and not the man who haunts my nightmares. He must have sensed me watching him because his eyes spring open, and he immediately moves his arms from my body. The sting of the loss is almost enough to bring those few tears from our kiss back, but I know there would be more because these would not be tears of happiness but ones of loss.

Quickly, I move away from him, and his eyes scrunch up, but other than that he gives nothing away. He's just watching me, and something in his gaze makes me feel like he's only doing this out of pity. I run into my room, close my door behind me, and lock it. Trembling, I slide down the door until I'm sitting on the floor. My eyes sting, begging me to give in, but I won't. Suddenly, something presses against the door and on the other side Cameron's breathing becomes heavy.

"Fate. I am so sorry," he says softly from behind my door.

"Leave," I say because if he keeps this up, I'm going to crack.

He hits the door, and I scream out as the impact bumps me off the door. "Fate, I'm so sorry. Please just open the door. I didn't mean to fall asleep. I'm sorry if I scared you when you woke up with my hands on you. I won't let it happen again if that's what you want."

What? Once I've turned around, I slowly turn the lock, crawl to the other side of the room away from the door, and press my back against the wall. "Come in," I whisper, and somehow he hears me. The door opens and the man before me is not the rock star I'm used to dealing with. All the confidence he usually has appears to have been stripped from him. He's lost and ashamed. Something that breaks me apart inside because I did this and I don't know what to say to fix it. I'm the problem and I don't know how to fix me.

"You didn't ask for any of this," I whimper, and he quickly cross the space between us. He is now bent down before me. I know he wants to touch me but is scared I'll pull away.

"I'm asking for this. Give me a chance to show you everything you deserve," he answers. "Fate, I'm sorry if I startled you. I let my anger with myself for touching you without permission get the better of me. I didn't mean to frighten you."

The pain in his face makes me push through my own. I grab the blanket beside me on my bed and wrap it around me. He just watches me as I push him slightly so that he is sitting down before me. Slowly, I crawl into his lap, making sure my skin is covered, having the blanket to act as a barrier between us. I hate that it is between us, but I know if I flinch or seem the slightest bit uncomfortable he'll know it and blame himself.

"Baby steps," I say, and he just smiles, agreeing with me as he holds me in his arms gently. If someone had told me I'd be here when I got to school, I would've told them to get their head checked, but here I am, feeling safe in the arms of another.

We sit like this for a while before I remember we have classes. Cameron seems happy to just sit here and miss school, but I'm not going to let him do that. He does try to persuade me.

WE MEET UP AT the end of the school day, and he asks me to come with him to a party. I tell him it isn't my thing, but Cecilia is there and she doesn't take no for an answer like Cameron does. So, here I sit in her bedroom, dressed but you'd think I was naked. My hair is curled, and I have makeup on. Gazing in the mirror, I don't even see *me* anywhere in the reflection before me. Cecilia assures me this is what everyone will be dressed like.

Waiting for the guys to come get us, Cecilia seems too excited, which makes my anxiety rise. "Cameron is going to flip shit when he sees you." I'm not sure if that is supposed to help my uncertainty but it only makes my feelings about this escalate.

A knock comes at the door and I'm almost ready to jump out of my skin. I make my way up the hallway of Cecilia's apartment, and stopping at the end, I lean against the wall. Feeling the need to have some support, I stay there and just peer at the floor. They come in; Scott and Cameron are both laughing, and then there is only silence.

"Come on, Cecilia, I need to pick something up at the store before we head out. We will be back to get you two in a few," Scott says, and I still don't glance up. As if everyone is watching me.

"If you make her feel anything other than a beautiful woman, I'm going to castrate you. I mean it, Cameron, it took me too long to get her to actually agree to this for you to screw with her." Cecilia sneer quietly, probably thinking I won't be able to hear her, but every word is clear. The door clicks and footsteps come toward me.

"I need you to change, Fate," he says, and I nod my head, turning to go back to the room I'd just come from. I'm such an idiot to think I can pull this off. His hand wraps around my wrist and I know he is staring at me. "Fate, look at me."

Slowly, my eyes connect with his. "I'm just going to do what you asked me to, Cameron. I'll be right back."

Walking ahead of me, he brings me with him into the back bedroom where my clothes are. He lets go of me and closes the door. He rakes his hand through his hair, and I finally take in his appearance. He is always attractive and something to be admired, but tonight it's like I'm more aware of him. Cameron has on a pair of dark-wash jeans that fit him perfectly. He's wearing a black button-up long sleeve shirt that shows off everything I love about his chest.

Cameron is just standing there staring at me. As I stare in the mirror next to us, I'm sure he is thinking the worst, that I don't have the same appearance as my previous self. My hair is falling down my back in big beautiful curls. I have on a black halter-top that exposes all of my back but two little straps. The bottom of it just reaches the black short skirt Cecilia demanded I wear. Plus, the fact that these heels make my legs appear lengthy, giving me height I've never had. I move to the bed where my clothes are, I grab them, but Cameron takes my hand in his, turns me back to him before letting go of me again. It's crazy how his touch has become something I welcome, although we only touch in baby steps.

"I'm just going to take my clothes and go get changed," I say quickly, but he just shakes his head at me. Slowly, I watch as his hand hovers over my skin, coming up my arm to where my shoulders are. There he lingers, never touching my skin, but the heat between us is undeniable.

"Fate, why do I want you to change?" he asks.

"Because this isn't who I am, I can't pull this off. I'm not this sexy party girl that Cecilia tried to make me into. My face is covered in makeup and my hair is perfect. It's very…not Fate," I say honestly and his hands move closer to my skin. Knowing I could just move slightly and we'd connect, I try to push those thoughts out of my head.

"That's half right. This isn't very you, but shit, you can pull it off. You're not a party girl, but you're damn sexy and the best part is you don't even know it. I'm not a fan of the makeup because you're right. It's covering everything I love to look at. Your hair is always perfect even when you've just rolled your adorable ass out of bed and you're grumbling the whole way to the fridge.

So that shit's moot. I need you to change because I want to touch you…" He pauses, and I use this moment to push my shoulder into the palm of his hand and his breath catches at the contact. He slowly begins to caress my shoulder and a trail of heat follow his hand as he moves it along my shoulder up to the back of my neck.

"Fate, everyone is going to be staring at you and it's going to drive me nuts. I'm going to want to make sure everyone knows you're mine so they stay the hell away from you. I know how you feel about public displays and touching. I just feel like I need you to cover up if we are going to go to this party."

On one hand, I feel as if I should be pinching myself, but my body also goes into a wild panic. He's a rock star. How long will these little touches hold him off before he wants more? Watching him, he leans in and I know what's coming. Meeting him, I gently place my lips against his and my body tighten as his mouth moves against mine. I tingle all over and I want to deepen the kiss, but I don't even know where to start. Gradually, I bring my hands up and wrap them around his waist, pulling him to me.

He breaks the kiss, leaning his forehead against mine, and his heavy breathing stuns me. "You're amazing," he says as if it's a matter of fact.

I pull him closer so he bumps against me. "I bet you tell that to all the girls."

He just shakes his head and moves out of my grasp. Cameron goes over to the closet; he grabs a black dressy jacket. He holds it out for me, and I put my arms in as he slips it on me. "That's better, now only I know what you look like from the back and I'll be thinking about that all night," he says without any joking tone in his voice and the temperature in my body rising. We grab our things and head out of the apartment in search of Scott and Cecilia, who are just waiting for us downstairs.

WHEN WE GET THERE, it's more like a club I'd imagine than a party. There is a D.J., dance floor, and a bar set up. Cameron leads us to a table, and Cecilia goes off in search of a bathroom. "Let's go get something to drink," Cameron says to Scott and me.

"I'll stay here and keep our spot. Nothing alcoholic for me," I say, and he smirks at me.

"Fine, I'll be watching you, and who do you think I am? I wouldn't supply a minor with alcohol," he says jokingly, and I swat at him playfully. "Don't leave this spot," he says firmly, and he grazes his fingers along mine before he takes off in the direction of the bar with Scott. At the bar, it's obvious that everyone is aware of him. The girls want him and the guys want to be him.

Someone comes in between my sight of him and tries to place something on Cameron's spot. "Sorry, that's my friend's spot, he just went to get drinks," I say politely, peeking at Cameron, who is now gazing over with a horrified expression on his face. When I glance back at the girl she is staring at me with distain, and I smirk at her, silently asking *who are you?*

"I'm the girlfriend, who the hell are you?"

Chapter Twelve

Cameron

IT'S AS IF MY life burns in front of my eyes. There standing in front of Fate was Trisha. I nudge Scott who turns, glancing back at the table, and he curses. The horror on Fate's face is pure agony. I have no clue what Trisha said to her, but I watch as Fate took off the jacket, threw it on the table and walked away, disappearing into the crowd.

Frantic to get to her, I shoulder my way through the throng of people and finally reach the table, but she's long gone. "Damn it," I yell.

Trisha turns, shooting me a menacing glare with a giant smile on her face. The pit of my stomach is churning, and I just want to run to Fate.

"Baby, there you are. Some girl was waiting here like a little groupie. She actually thought you went to get her a drink. Don't worry, baby, I set her straight." Leaning into me, she tries to kiss me. I don't even have a chance to move, because from behind her, Fate and her eyes connect with mine just as Trisha's lips touch the side of my mouth. The anguish showing on Fate's face damn near wrecks me.

What the hell have I done? Pushing Trisha back gently, I shift my eyes down at her with worry. "What did you say to her?" I say abruptly. I signal Scott telling him to go off and find Fate. He motions his hands for me to deal with this shit and goes off in the direction I just saw her flee to. "Trisha, what the hell did you do?" I snap.

"I told her I was the girlfriend and put her in her place. I don't care if you're flirting with your little fans, but when I'm here they need to realize who comes first," she says proudly, and my rage builds. Not just at Trisha but at myself. I should have told her about Trisha before any of this happened because that would have made this so much easier to explain when I finally catch up to her.

"You had no right," I growl while grabbing Fate's jacket. I take off to where I just saw Scott disappear, leaving Trisha behind. After fighting my way through the crowd, I finally get outside, and my heart drops to the ground when she speaks.

"I should have known. I'm so stupid," she screams at Cecilia, who is trying to calm her down. "He's a freaking rock star, and I'm just some freshman with nothing to offer him." Scott is just looking at Fate, and I know he is feeling helpless in all this. "I'm leaving. I am not going back in there. When I get back to the apartment, I'm packing my stuff and going home for the weekend. I need some space. He should have told me, Cecelia," she shouts.

"Yes, he should have. I told you he's an asshole and you'd need me to bitch to, but be fair, there are two sides to every story, Fate," Cecilia says, clearly trying to bring Fate back from the rage she is feeling.

"Either you have a girlfriend or you don't. It's that fucking easy!" she roars, and I flinch at her swearing. This girl doesn't curse, and I did this. All that anger and hurt is because I didn't tell her about Trisha.

"She's not my girlfriend," I declare as I come up behind her.

"Does she know that? I think she is and you're just saying this now because you got caught, Cameron," she shrieks at me, and I've never seen her so angry. Not even when I nailed the neighbor.

"You're right, I do have a girlfriend," I confess and she gasps. Cecilia is screaming at me that I'm a damn idiot, and Scott is saying that I'm an asshole. Trying to clear them out of this equation, I walk up to Fate and attempt to touch her, but she smacks me away.

"Don't you dare touch me, Cameron McAlister. You will never touch me again. Do you hear me? Never," she continues shouting at me. "I hate you."

Watching her walk away with Cecilia trying to comfort her, it's as if I'm losing my mind. "She is this sexy and amazing person. This girl just came up and saw me for the real me not some fake rock star and I'm sorry for that."

Scott turns on me and I think he might actually punch me. "You are not helping, just shut up," he shouts at me.

"She talks about these incredible facts and has inspired so much in me that I just don't know what I'd do without her." Turning, Fate's eyes lock with mine and there are tears streaming down her face. I want to go to her, but I have to get this out before it's too late. "She tells me about her love of fish and her thoughts on the world. She lets me in and shuts the rest of the world out. She'll never know how much she means to me. I hate that my past taints her because I'd give anything to protect her from it."

My own eyes are betraying me as the sting from the raw emotions setting in. "Her name is Fate McKenzie, and I am falling in love with her so hard that I don't think I'd ever recover if I couldn't touch her, hold her, and, if she hated me, that would kill me," I say as I start taking steps toward her. Cecilia is watching this whole thing and I'm not sure if she's going to get in my way, but right now, I need Fate. "Because I need her as much as I hope she needs me," I whisper when I'm close enough to her.

"Baby, there you are."

Are you kidding me, Trisha? This girl's timing is going to be the death of me. Quickly, I turn and put myself in front of Fate, hoping to protect her from Trisha.

"What is this?" Trisha says snidely, and I want to run away, taking Fate with me. "I thought we covered this. I'm the girlfriend, so run along now."

"Trisha, that's where you are wrong. I'm sorry you have to find out this way, but you really didn't leave much choice when you walked up to my girlfriend and tried to act as if we haven't been broken up for eight damn months."

Her face turns to anger and she glances around me at Fate. "Oh, and this is my replacement? Let's be serious now, she's not even twenty, I'd bet," Trisha says spitefully.

"Eighteen," Fate squeaks out.

"Oh, that's precious. You can't be serious, Cam." She walks closer and Fate presses against my back. I wrap my arms behind me, holding her waist against me. "Honey, you're way out of your league here. Do yourself a favor and back out gracefully before you make an even bigger fool of yourself. I have two years of history with this man. You can't compete with that." Fate gasps and she tries to pull away from me.

"You are such a bitch," Cecilia yells at Trisha. "Don't stand there acting like you have all this shit with him. You're just acting that way to scare Fate off, and hell, I'm not about to let that happen. Two years, that's a laugh. On and off for two years, most of the time off, trust me, Fate. This girl is just jealous that he's found someone she can't hold a candle to. Sorry, but you just missed the show, sweetheart. He just told her he's falling in love with her. I know for damn sure he never said shit like that to you."

Thank you, Cecilia.

"Cam? Is this true?" Trisha says.

"Not that what I have with Fate is any of your damn business, but yes. If she will have me, then I'm hers. You're done here," I say, hoping this will show her that she has no chance.

"Well then, keep the tramp. I know the drill." Her words are filled with hate toward Fate and that makes my blood boil. I watch as she walks around so she is in complete view of Fate. "I bet you think I'm crazy, Fate. Just wait and see what I do to you. You're just some little pawn in his new game. All screwed up, needing a hero. That will get old and he will return to me. You just wait and see. He always does," Trisha says, then turns and walks away, leaving a stunned Fate behind.

I don't know what to do or what to say right now to Fate. "Cameron, you should get Fate home." Cecilia suggests. I nod and go to hand Fate the jacket, and she flinches. I can't tell you how much her doing that is killing me right now. She turns and begins to walk in the direction of our apartment. I follow her, nodding a goodbye to Cecilia and Scott, who are watching me with pity. *I'm so fucking screwed right now.*

When we enter the apartment, Fate heads to her room. I rush ahead of her, blocking the door, forcing her to peek up at me. "I'm exhausted, Cameron."

"It's dark, you can't sleep in there and you know it," I say, hoping it works, and I place my hands on her waist and lead her to the couch. She doesn't resist, and I sense she is just giving in to the motions. "Fate, say something."

"When was the last time you two were together… sexually?" she asks with such innocence; I hate that my past has her having to ask this question.

"It's been almost nine months since I've had anything sexual with her. She pops up from time to time and likes to play the girlfriend of the rock star. I never cared before because I didn't want anyone in my life. It was easier to say nothing," I say truthfully.

"Other than tonight, when you kissed." Of course, to her that appeared sexual.

"Fate, she kissed me on the side of my mouth. The only reason I didn't move away was because I was watching you. I didn't even know what was happening until it was too late and I pushed her off me as soon as she tried." She bites her lip in response. I know she's confused. I am too. I thought we had something here, maybe it's one sided. "Fate, do you want to be with me?" I ask her, praying she doesn't rip me wide open.

"If we do this, it has to be just me. I'm not her, I never will be. This will be all about baby steps, and I can't even promise you anything sexual because I've never done most of the things you have." Her words cut me.

"Have I ever done anything to make you think I needed more from you?" She shakes her head. "Was it something I said? Did I say something to make you think I wanted her or anyone else and not you?" I thought I was being clear about my feelings for her.

"You make it seem as if I'm everything, and that is amazing but also overwhelming. It's like nothing I've ever felt before, which is both thrilling and horrifying. I'm new to all this, but the way you make me feel is like together we can handle anything," she says, peering up at the ground again. I bring her chin up forcing her gaze lock with mine.

"That's because I'm all about you, only you, so let's give this another try."

Chapter Thirteen

Fate

When I come through the door, Cameron is sitting on the couch with his guitar. As soon as he sees me, he quickly goes to his room and puts it away. I've never caught him doing this before, but I know he listens to music when I'm not around and sneaks around to practices with the band. I didn't even notice he had a guitar in his room when I'd been in there. He must have it tucked away somewhere. When he comes out, I decide that we need to find some way of moving past this.

"I was wondering if you'd be interested in doing something with me," I say timidly, and he cocks his eyebrow at me in response. "No, not that. Well, we have different interests, and I was thinking maybe we could do something for each other that the other person enjoys." He chuckles and I realize that could still be taken badly. "Ugh, you're such a man. You know what I mean. Stop making this about that," I say in a frustrated but joking tone.

"I'm game," Cameron says, and I smile because I wasn't sure if he'd go for something like this.

"You have to trust me," I say, because I'm sure I'll

get some hesitation from him at some point.

"I think that's fair since I'm always asking you to trust me and take baby steps. Now it's your turn," he says to me with a smile, and it warms my heart that he's so carefree. What I wouldn't give to feel that way. "So, tell me, Fate, what is something I don't enjoy already by being around you that you could share with me?"

Crap. I hadn't thought about something like that. "Fish," I blurt out. *Great job, Fate*. "I mean, you know I love nature, but I have a huge passion for marine life."

"Why, though? Is it just because you are a nature lover or is there something else behind it?"

I hadn't expected him to ask anything about it. Honestly, if someone had blurted out what I had, I'd think they were a little crazy, but for some reason he can sense where reasons are with me. "When my mom died it was something I dove into. My earliest memory with my mom was going to the zoo. I remember walking into the fish exhibit and my mom was so excited that I was interested in it. Before she passed away I even wanted to be a marine biologist," I say, knowing I exposed more than I had planned too.

"So why are you here studying Law?" he questions as if I'm either going to have to lie or be honest.

"Life happened," I say, trying to be vague, but he glances at me, telling me I won't be getting away with it that easily. "I could have stayed in Florida, studied there and probably never have had to move away from Clarissa. But I needed to start over. I don't want to go back to Orlando. I want to find a new place in the world for me. Marine life is important to me, but after my mom died, it became more of a passion for me to get away. Then something about Law called to me too.

I chose Law and a new life. I want to be able to help people and this is my way." I am being honest. I just omitted certain parts of it. Sometimes things are better left unsaid.

"I can understand that. So fish…what do you want me to do for your part then?"

I try to think of something quickly but nothing comes. The only thing I can think of is one of my books. Leaving him for a moment, I go into my room and grab the book. Sitting in front of him, I hand him the book. "My mom got me this for my birthday before she died. It has a bit of everything in it about marine life, not just fish. You don't have to read it all or any. Maybe just check out the pictures. There are some very beautiful things in this world."

Cameron brings his hand up to my face and cups my cheek in his hand. Instinctively I lean into his touch, and he smiles at my ease. "Yes, there are," he whispers to me, and my heartbeat quickens. "Okay, so I'll do this, but I'm not sure what you could do for me," he states and I already know what I want to do, but I'm hoping he will bring it up, then maybe he won't be so hesitant.

"What are you passionate about?" I say, hinting, but of course, Cameron has to be snarky.

"You," he says in a serious tone. My body feels the need to squirm under his gaze, and he just continues staring at me.

"I'm serious, Cameron," I say.

"I didn't lie to you, Fate," he says plainly.

"I've learned sometimes it's best to not argue with you. What else are you passionate about?" I can see the hesitation in his face, and he's staring at me. He knows

I want him to say it, but he just can't.

"Fate, you know what else I'm passionate about. I can't ask you to have anything to do with music," he declares, and the fact that this man is always protecting me is heartwarming.

"Baby steps," I reply, and he wavers, maybe trying to find something he can do that will appease me.

"Well, you've already read my lyrics, so I'm not sure what else I can share with you," Cameron says, and I can tell he is searching within himself for something to share with me that won't cause me harm. He just won't go to the obvious with me, leaving me no choice but to be the bold one.

"Can I go into your room?" I ask, and he gives me a questioning smirk. "Maybe something will jump out at me since you're not sure what to share," I say, hoping he will agree. When he nods I squeeze his hand tightly and go in search of our next baby step.

When I walk into his room, it screams Cameron. There are musical charts on the walls and I even see he has a poster of the band. I search for it, but I can't see it anywhere. *Where would he hide it?* I know he wouldn't want me to accidentally find it, so the only place is under the bed, and when I crawl down there, right in front of me is the case. I drag it out from under the bed and carry it out to the living room. When he sees it, he's already shaking his head at me.

"No way, Fate. I know how you are with music. You may not have completely said it, but it's a damn trigger and you're asking me to pull it. Why?"

That's a good question, and to be honest, I really don't know. I just feel as if I need this. "Cameron, music is so much of your life. It's like I'm missing out on pieces of you, and I hate that. You said you'd trust me. Well, I want this. Let me hear you play." Opening the case, I finally get to check out his guitar. It's an acoustic guitar in a stunning blue shade with the name Les Paul written on it. Carefully, I pick it up and hand it to him.

"Are you sure?"

No, I'm not, but I have to try. Cameron deserves this from me. "Yes," I whisper, but instead of playing he goes to my room and comes back holding something I hadn't thought about since the day I met him. He opens the package and hands them to me, and I glance at him for direction.

"I want you to put these in."

Confusion takes over. I thought the point was to hear him play. "I won't be able to hear you. It defeats the purpose," I state, and he appears so different right now with his guitar. It's as if I'm actually getting a chance to see Cameron the rocker and not just Cameron my roommate, whom I'm falling for.

"Trust me," he says, and I give him a smirk. Sneaky man using my words against me. He knows I have no choice but to agree. When I nod, he sets the guitar down beside him on the couch and he puts out his hand for me to come to him. I go with ease and turn around, sitting in his lap. He motions for me to put the earplugs in. Once he's checked that I can barely hear anything, he makes sure we are both comfortable. I watch as he grabs his guitar and brings it in front of me against my chest. His hands move, and I can't hear what he's doing but something else is happening.

It's beautiful and so much more than I thought I'd get from this experience with him. I can't help the few tears that fall. He continues and I watch his hand move across the strings. The vibrations against my chest give me a beat, but I'm not hearing it. It's as if he found a way around my trigger in this moment. He knew how to do this better than I did. Cameron continues for what seems like hours, and I just sit there against him. I would have continued to sit there, but he eventually stops and puts the guitar down beside us. Pulling out my earplugs, he stares at me and he can see how moved I am by this.

"Was that too hard?" he asks softly.

"No, that was perfect. Another perfect baby step," I say with an adoring smile on my face. This man is mine, and he is absolutely amazing.

"You're exhausted," he says, and the fatigue sets in. "Do you think you could try sleeping on the couch again with the lights on?" he asks, and I nod. He puts his guitar away and goes to get bedding. He sets up the bed, and when he goes to try to tuck me in, something is different. A new need takes over, a new thing I need to comfort me at night.

"Will you lie with me?" I ask, and his face turns to shock. He appears so unsure, so I get up and motion for him to lie down. When he finally does, I take one of the blankets and hand it to him. I grab the other one and wrap it around me, making sure all my skin is covered. Then I lie down next to him. I can tell he doesn't know what to do with his arms. He just seems so stiff and unlike Cameron. "Cameron, you can touch me," I say, and slowly his arm slides across me and he pulls me closer.

"Thank you," he whispers.

"For what?"

"The music, telling me about your mom, but mostly

for this."

I snuggle back into him, making sure the only thing between us is the blanket.

"I think my fate might be sealed," he whispers against me, and I don't have to question him. I know he's talking about us, and I think he might be right.

Chapter Fourteen

Cameron

GETTING USED TO SLEEPING with the lights on actually wasn't that big of a problem for me. Lying next to Fate, I didn't give a damn about what was going on around us. She took it all away. I can't believe how far she's come and she finally trusts me. Fate believes in me. I know that sounds conceited, but it's not. This girl doesn't trust anyone, so this is a huge accomplishment in my books. She's been trying to venture off a bit more by herself during the day. She doesn't always eat lunch with me at school anymore, much to my protest. Some shit about baby steps. Whose idea was that? *Oh right, mine. I'm an idiot.*

I never thought baby steps would come with a disadvantage for me, but she found a way. So here I sit, watching her from across the room as she interacts with some people from her class. It's amazing really, because you wouldn't think she is this broken person right now. She's also oblivious to the fact that everyone is drawn to her. On each side of her is another guy. As long as they keep their hands to themselves, I won't have any problems.

Fate is laughing at something, and these assholes are just sitting there watching her. She doesn't even know how beautiful she is. She tries to blend in, but this damn girl was born to stand out. She glances over in my direction, and when our eyes meet, she blushes; I love that I do that to her. It never gets old how little I've touched this girl, but yet her body responds to me.

The guys don't seem to notice; in fact, it appears as if one of them seems to think that redness on her face is thanks to him. When Fate's attention turns to the guy on the other side of her, he pulls his chair closer to hers. Turning back, Fate doesn't seem to notice, but I do. He hands her his phone and it seems like he's trying to get her number.

I can't just sit here and watch this, so I stand and make my way over to where she is, the whole time hoping she will see me coming so I don't have to interrupt her or put her on the spot. She never does, though. She is just staring at the phone, but she hasn't put her number in yet. Once I come up behind her, I make sure I don't touch her before I get her attention. "Fate," I say, and she turns to me smiling.

"Cameron," she says, and I can see the guys getting pissed that I'm talking to her. I want to tell them to screw off and leave her alone because she's mine, but I think that a pissing contest would just further submerge my girl in her shell. One I am so desperately trying to get her out of.

"I'm going back to *our* apartment, and I wondered if you wanted to walk with me," I say, hoping these guys get the hint. When they hear that we live together, they both change from the angry grimaces I was getting, telling me I was intruding on their game, to an *oh shit, better not go there* glance.

"That would be great." She puts her stuff together quickly and gets out of the chair. "I'll see you guys later," she says.

As we walk away, I can't help the urge to touch her. "Fate?" I hold my hand out for her to take it. She doesn't question it, she just puts her hand in mine, continuing to walk away. It takes everything in me not to turn the hell around and check to make sure those dumbasses see that she's mine.

When we get to the apartment, I have this urge to come clean about why I interrupted her time with her friends, even though she's not questioning my intentions. "I hope you're not pissed that I took you away from your friends," I say, and she just shakes her head. "I couldn't just sit there and watch those guys vying for your attention."

"What are you talking about?" she says, completely clueless.

"The one guy moved closer to you and then tried to get your number, right?" I ask, and it all click together for her. "Watching that and not being able to say back off she's mine was a task. So I just got you out of there."

"You were jealous?" she questions, and I want to shake this girl because she just doesn't get it.

"Of course I'm jealous that I can't yell it from the rooftops that I'm with you. I don't like men coming around what's mine." She gives me a glare, and I worry I've said too damn much. *Shit.*

"What's yours? Am I a possession?"

I don't even know what to say. I just stand there scared shitless that I'm going to say the wrong thing, then my girl busts out laughing.

"Oh my God, you should have seen your face, Cameron."

"You were just screwing with me?" I ask seriously.

"Cameron, have you ever seen me touch anyone else?" she questions.

I shake my head in response because I'm not sure what this girl is feeling. Is she mad at me for what I've said, or is she just giving me a hard time? "Never."

"Then that should tell you who I belong to," she announces. "Is that why you wanted to hold my hand, to show them?"

"Not entirely. Part of me wanted them to see it. The other part of me just had this overwhelming urge to touch you," I say truthfully.

"I get that way too," she confesses, and I reach out to her. "So then we should just do what our bodies are telling us to. If you want to touch me, then do it. Just only in ways we've already done, okay? I'll do the same." She hesitates.

"Thank fuck," I say, and she laughs but turns serious again.

"Cameron, don't kiss me in public. I'm not ready for the staring yet. Here, I know it's just you and me, but out there, I just don't want the attention." The fact that she even thought she had to tell me this makes me feel uneasy.

"Fate, I would never do that to you. No matter what urge I got. I won't take that step until you show me you're ready." She leans in and presses her soft lips lightly against mine. Feeling this with her, I can't blame her for not wanting to do it in public. I know if I were a guy seeing her kiss someone, I'd either be watching, pissed that it wasn't me, or turned on. This also means that no one but me gets to see this side of Fate, and that's sexy as hell.

"I have something for you," I say and go into my room to grab it. Coming out, I hope she doesn't get mad that I went and bought her this. I just want to try something new. Handing her the rectangular box, I can see she is confused by it. When she opens it, she appears happy, but I still don't think she gets the purpose of them. "Do you know why I bought those for you?"

"Because you have a thing with me and pajamas?" she says as she glances at each pajama onesie I had put into the box. "Really, what is with you and kitties?" She laughs as she draws her forefinger along the back of one of the kittens. "I mean three different patterns?"

"First impressions," I say jokingly, and she smiles at me. This time the smile touches her eyes and I know it's real. "Do you understand why I got you this particular kind?" She shakes her head in response. "Well, for the past couple of weeks we have been sleeping together on the couch. Same drill every night." She nods, and I continue, "So I thought maybe if I got you something that covered most of you that you might feel less worried. Maybe you wouldn't need to wrap yourself up so snuggly."

It's as if a light clicks on, and she's put the pieces together. "Another baby step," she says with a smile, and I return it. This girl has made me into a damn wimp, and I don't even give a shit.

"So, do you think you could do that?" I ask, hoping I didn't just set things back for her.

"I think so, maybe every few nights I could wear something with a bit more skin." She slaps her hands over her mouth, and I break out in a chuckle.

"Well, that sounds good too," I say jokingly, and she just shakes her head, laughing with me.

"What I meant is maybe it wouldn't be such a big deal for me if I did it in stages. Does that make sense?"

I can't help the feeling of knowing this could lead me to have more access to her and be able to touch her more. She needs this; for that reason, I don't have a problem being with her the way it is. I already know I'm wrecked for the rest of the world. Fate is it for me. "I know what you mean, Fate. Baby steps," I say to her with a wink, and she giggles.

She grabs one of the kitty onesies and quickly gives me a kiss, then takes off to her room to get changed, I presume. When she walks out, I can see she's trying to not laugh at her appearance. There is my beautiful girl, standing in the pajamas I got her and they even have those funny feet parts too. She is covered everywhere, except her hands and face, her safe zones that she has no issues with. I have noticed I can touch her in other areas, but when it comes to sleeping, it's a different game plan. It's as if this is her most stressful time, and she reverts back to that shit we were dealing with weeks ago.

"I look like an idiot," she says, kicking her covered foot against the floor.

Getting up, I walk over to her and slide my hand in hers. "You look like someone who's going to keep me warm," I say with a smirk on my face. "I get to sleep with you without you being wrapped up like a little bug. I get to feel your hands and touch your face. You could be wearing anything and I'd be thankful because tonight I get to touch you," I say as I lead her to the couch that I'd made up while she was getting changed.

Quickly, I lie down and she follows me without hesitation. I wait for her to turn around, but tonight she doesn't. "What is it?" I ask because she just keeps staring at me.

"I want to try something since I'm covered." My interested is piqued, and I wait for her to continue. "Take off your shirt," she says, and I hesitate.

"Fate, what are you doing?"

"Just do it, McAlister," she says with such attitude, it's hard not to laugh at her. She isn't usually one to be this way, and when she is, I'm either fighting back laughter or turned on. Tonight, I have to admit it's a bit of both. *Damn.* Slowly, I sit up and begin lifting my shirt because I'm scared she's going to change her mind and it will become too much for her, but she doesn't stop me.

She just continues to stare at me, and I can't help but love the way she is staring at my bare chest. I know she's attracted to me. I love when she enjoys the view, as she should. It's for her eyes only.

Chapter Fifteen

Fate

"Hello?"

"Oh, Fate. I'm glad I caught you," she says quickly.

Clarissa's voice tells me something is up right away. "What's wrong, Clarissa? Are you okay?"

"Honey, I'm fine, but I can't come for Thanksgiving. I'm sorry."

My heart sinks. The thought of not seeing her has my heart beating out of control. I won't make her worse by telling her how brokenhearted I am. There is no point in making her feel dismal about it. She can't help it. Kids like me need workers like her.

"It's okay, there's always Christmas." I reply, trying to sound as cheery as possible.

"I got you a ticket, you just have to pick it up at the airport on your way here." At first I'm overjoyed by her response then my stomach twists when I realize this means I won't be seeing Cameron. "I can't wait to see you."

I'm torn. I want to ask Cameron to come with me, but I know Clarissa isn't going to be thrilled with this arrangement. Until now I never realized how much I cared for Cameron.

"I HATE THAT YOU'RE leaving," Cameron says, and he can't even keep a little smile on his face. It's as if someone came and sucked out all his happiness, and I'm right there with him. "You should stay. We will tell Clarissa you got sick and shouldn't travel," he says hopefully, and the idea does sound amazing, but I can't do that to Clarissa.

"It will only be five days, Cameron. Not a big deal. Just about three months ago, I didn't even exist in your world. Go off and do rock star things. I can't leave Clarissa alone. She doesn't have anyone but me. I'm all the family she has," I say softly.

"Shit. I don't like this, but I won't beg you to stay. I know you need to see her and you should. Damn, how did this happen?" I gaze at Cameron questioningly because I don't know what he means. "This. Us. It just came up behind me. Five days is going to be torture. Three months ago I didn't know what I was missing, now I do and it blows." He sulks and I can't help but hug him. He wraps his arms around me, and it brings my body back to life like each of his touches do. The chaos of the airport has me in knots thinking about the days to come.

It's time for me to go through security and leave him behind. My body has this overwhelming sense of sorrow. I had kissed him before we left the apartment and I wanted to try to do it here, but the fear paralyzes me. The only comfort I can get from him is his touch, so I soak it all in. "I have to go," I whisper, and he holds me tighter, then reluctantly let's go. As I move away, my hand stays connected to his until the last moment. Just as my hand drops, I take a deep breath, trying to fight through the disconnect. "Five days," I whisper and turn, rushing off.

Here I am two days later, exhausted and miserable because other than text messages and phone calls, I couldn't fit anything else in with Clarissa. The reason she couldn't come was because she couldn't get off work. She was on call and that meant she was getting called away every few hours. I didn't mind, though. I just used that time to talk to Cameron, but when night came I fell back into old habits. Clarissa, of course, thought nothing of it since she didn't know any better until she saw how tired I was.

"Are you really okay, Fate? You're more exhausted every hour you are here. When I saw you get off the plane you just appeared so rested, and now you are worse than before you left for school." Clarissa has been able to read me pretty well since the day we met. It was her job, but now she has years of getting to know me, and she can tell when I'm keeping things from her.

"I miss Cameron," I say honestly.

"I'm not sure if I like you being so serious about someone, especially someone like him." Her words cut me. Clarissa is always honest, that's what I like most about her, but it hurts to hear.

"Why, because he's a rock star instead of going to medical school?" I can't help the attitude that comes out. Never before have I felt as if I was being attacked by Clarissa, but she's talking about Cameron. My Cameron, who has helped me through everything. *He doesn't deserve it. Judgment.*

"I would have the same concerns about him either

way. Have you read about him? It's not pleasant." Her words are hurtful.

"He's not perfect, but he is trying. I'm not perfect and you know that. So why would you think a perfect guy is what I need? Do you even know what he's done for me? No, you don't because you don't ask. All you're doing is judging him, Clarissa. I never thought you'd be so judgmental," I yell, frightening her.

"What has he done?"

"Now you want to know? Why should I tell you? So you could use it against us again?" I declare, and she peers at me with surprise.

"I didn't know there was an 'us.' I think I'm now more worried about the fact that you didn't tell me about that than what is out there about him." She gives me a concerned smile, which only makes me angrier.

"I know what's out there. It's not a secret."

"But you are a secret," she says, and I know she is worried about the implications of me dating him. "I don't just mean I don't want you publically out there for the world. I mean he hasn't come out and said anything about you." The sting from her words penetrates my walls. "How much could he really care about you?"

"That's not fair, Clarissa. It's all new. We haven't even labeled it anything. How could it be possible for us to go public if I'm not even sure exactly what we are?" I say, straining to make her see my way, but I can't help the thought that maybe Cameron doesn't want people to know about me. I know he referred to me as his girlfriend at the party, but I'm not sure that was a declaration of his perception of us or if it was just him attempting to get through to me. That hurts the most. I've been back here two days and Clarissa has made me doubt it.

"But there is a 'we' of some sort?"

"Yes. I can't speak for him, but I would say that it's more than that for me at least," I say honestly, and she gasps.

"You can't date a rock star with his history. What about the touching?"

Her words bring me back to our moments in the apartment; I only miss him more now. "Cameron knows."

Clarissa just stares at me. "You told him," she says finally, and I know she doesn't believe that I would.

"He knows that someone hurt me. That it has left an effect on me, and my issues with touching and the dark. He is amazing, patient with me, and does not push when he knows I'm struggling. He's…Cameron," I say, and I know that each word is truth.

"What happens when he finds out?"

"Then I hope we will deal with it together, but I hope he never does find out. If he leaves, then I will have to live with the consequences of my actions." I take a deep breath, but I can't seem to calm myself. So I think back to every baby step. "I'm telling you he's different. He is able to handle my issues," I finally say when I'm able to get a grip on myself again.

"That will only last so long. Men have needs, same as your need for a slow pace. He will want more and you may feel pressured." She watches me and again takes in my appearance. "Please tell me you haven't had sex with him already and this is why you're the way you are right now."

"Are you serious? Not that I have to tell you

anything, but we haven't had sex. The reason I'm like this is because I'm back here and without him. I sleep with him every night and we don't even have to keep all the lights on."

Clarissa inhales sharply. "This is very concerning to me. You're far too involved and dependent on this young man already. To top it off, you live together. I know I've been positive about this relationship, but all this new information has me concerned. What happens when he loses interest?" She sees the hurt in my face and tries to repair the damage. "Not that I think he should, you know. I think anyone would be lucky to have you, but history shows he doesn't do commitment."

I can't exactly show her anything to change her mind, so I go for the shock factor just to shut her up. "History shows that I'm something too, does it not? So, let's just drop it."

Clarissa is hurt by my words and she opens her mouth as if to speak, but something— maybe my expression— makes her change her mind. She leaves, and I know she has to get away to either cry or calm down. I'd feel horrible if my heart wasn't hurting at the thought of Cameron leaving me.

Clarissa comes in a short time later and has the mail in her hand. She hands it to me, and I swipe through it. My name is on one, and the return address… My body runs ice cold. I open it, quickly reading through it, and the further in I get into the letter, the more nauseated I get.

"Fate, what's wrong?" Clarissa begs, and I just shake my head.

This can't be happening, not now. This is something

I knew would happen one day, but staring at the letter I don't think I ever really prepared myself for it. "He's getting released."

Chapter Sixteen

Cameron

NOTHING WAS GOING RIGHT in my world. I couldn't study worth shit because I kept thinking about Fate. Being in the apartment was even worse because I could see her everywhere. She was all around the campus, so I packed some of my stuff and left. I went to Scott's parents for some family bonding.

The whole time I was distracted, and his mom, Terry, kept busting my balls about it. She stopped when Scott let it slip that I was missing a girl. Then all the questions ensued about what she was like, which only made things worse. I told them everything I could think of. Scott called me a pussy, and his mom smacked him. They want me to bring her around at Christmas, and nothing would make me happier. I can't do this distance thing with her anymore, and I don't give a shit what that says about me.

Music wasn't even enough to keep my mind off her. I still kept my headphones on even though she wasn't there. It just felt as if she could still hear it. Bringing her pain is something I just can't do, so it became a habit to keep my headphones on. I tried working on the new album, but that just made it worse because the only thing I could write about was Fate.

When Fate stops calling me and making excuses for missing my calls, I got this horrible feeling in the pit of my stomach. She continues to text me, but only if I text her first. She doesn't ignore my text messages, but they weren't the same. Something is different, and it is killing me. I am sleeping like crap without her in my arms. I'm told by the band that makes me one testy shithead to deal with. They cancelled the extra practices I'd set up after I found out my girl was leaving for five days. Something had to keep my mind off her being so far away, but none of it had works. I need to see her. To hold her. To breathe in her sweet warm scent and know my world is not crumbling before me.

"Cameron? What are you doing here?" The woman before me is not how I was picturing Clarissa. She is taller than Fate and has black hair. Her eyes are dark, and she is wearing a dressy outfit. She's nothing I imagined my Fate was raised around. I know she isn't Fate's mom, but usually there are still similar things: like clothing or the way someone holds themselves. But all I'm getting off this woman is that she is a force to be reckoned with.

"You must be Clarissa. It's nice to finally meet you," I say politely, hoping to change the grimace on her face.

"Cameron, this isn't a good time. You should just see Fate when she gets back to school." Her eyes are trying to tell me something, but I don't know them to pick up on it. Whatever it is, though, it only makes my need to see Fate that much stronger.

"Where is she?"

"She's resting, Cameron. It's not a good day, and I just don't know how much she can handle. Another time this would be a wonderful surprise, but maybe tomorrow, okay?" she says, and I just want to push past her and find Fate, but that will only make her hate me and that's not going to help my cause.

"I knew something was wrong. She's not answering my calls at all anymore. I had to come." Damn, I should have just asked to come with her like I wanted to, then I wouldn't be out here in the cold when I have this overwhelming feeling that Fate needs me.

"Cameron, you can't help her right now."

I hate that this person who is so important to Fate is telling me this. Making me feel as if I'm in the way. "Is she okay?" I ask, and Clarissa shakes her head. "What happened, Clarissa?" I beg. "What the hell happened? It has only been four days."

"I can't tell you. It's not my story to tell. You know about some of her history, but what's happening right now isn't something she wants to share or she would have told you, Cameron." The truth behind her words burns me to my core.

"Maybe she was scared or wanted to tell me in person." Taking a breath, I try to calm my shit, my body going into hyper drive as if everything is falling apart. "Or maybe she never tells me, but that doesn't mean I can't be there for her."

"You can't force her," Clarissa says, giving me a look that says, *I'll mess you up if you try.*

"I won't. I just need to see her, please." I'd get on my hands and knees right now if I thought it would get me in the door.

"Fine." Her phone starts ringing, and she sighs.

"That's work, which means I have to go. Take care of her and, most of all, listen to her. I'll be back as soon as I can. Let me tell Fate you're here."

"No, I can. I know that if you're getting a call it must be important. If she wants me to leave, I will leave. I won't make her see me if its causing her pain. I just need to see her for a moment." I say.

After a moment's hesitation, Clarissa nods and points down the hall, quickly grabbing her stuff before heading out of the house.

When I get to the end of the hall, I know I've found the right room because every light is on. Walking in, I almost stumble when she comes into view. She is nothing like the girl I put on the plane four days ago. It's like the shell of her is in lying front of me.

"What are you doing here?" she says, and it kills me that it's not in a happy way.

"I wanted to see you." As I reach out to touch her, she flinches and moves away from me. Something has ripped through the girl I care about, and I don't even know what to do to help her. I'm hoping she will talk to me.

"I'm coming back tomorrow night," she says snidely.

"I thought we could go back together, and I wanted to spend time with you away from school. I'd thought maybe you could show me around," I say hopefully. Honestly, I don't give a damn if we leave this room, I just need to be with her. When she says nothing and doesn't move toward me as she usually would, I have no choice. "What happened, Fate?"

"Nothing," she screams at me, and my soul is being twisted. Something is very wrong here.

"Okay, if you don't want to tell me, that's fine. We don't have to talk about it. We can talk about what we are going to do over Christmas break. I was thinking I could take you to meet Scott's Family, well, my family." Maybe if I change the subject I can pull her from whatever it is that is bothering her. Put her focus on us and not all this shit that's weighing her down.

"You deserve to be with someone you can love." I don't know where that came from. She could barely even say 'love,' and I think I finally come to terms with how decimated this girl is. Doesn't change a thing for me, though. Why can't she see how amazing she is?

"And you think I won't?" I want to just come out and say it, but she's like a deer caught in the headlights. I have to approach her cautiously right now.

"You can't," she yells, jumping out of the bed away from me, scaring the shit out of me. Not even when she's in her nightmares have I ever seen her this shaken.

"But I do." I have no choice now. She's putting those brick walls up, and I can't get to her unless she lets me. Hopefully, telling her she will now let me in.

"No," she screams. "It's not allowed. Do you hear me? Never."

"Why are you acting this way?" I want to shake her and yell 'just tell me what the hell is wrong,' but that won't get us anywhere. I can't even get angry because I have this sense of dread settling over me.

"This is just the way I am. Stop trying to fix me."

It's as if a truck just ran me down, backed up, and did it again. "Why would I fix you? There is nothing wrong with you, Fate," I plead. I don't care if she's always in pieces, I will take them all.

"If you believe that, then you are sadly mistaken."

Those words make the hair on the back of my neck stand up. Walking around the bed, I try to go to her, hoping our touch will calm her the same way it does at home, but she puts her hands up, halting me.

"I'm not what you need. I wish I was, but I'm not. So it's done. Finished," she demands, and I lose my mind. How is this happening? Where is the girl who told me off and made me bow down to her? The girl before me just so defeated.

"Don't say that. You're upset and that's okay, but don't push me away." I would sell my soul just to take her pain away right now. Screw my pain, I'd give anything to save her from the anguish she's in right now.

"Go," she yells, and the pain I'm getting from her is torture. I'm not just feeling my heart being demolished, but her pain is damn well knocking me out.

"I'll go, if that's what you really want, Fate," I say, pleading to her with my eyes to tell me to stay.

"I want you to leave."

Shit. I should have listened to Clarissa. "But I love you." This girl just crippled me. If she's going to leave me, she needs to know. Not just because I want her to stay, because it's the Goddamn truth. This girl consumes me.

"You could obliterate me, Cameron, don't you understand that?" Does this girl not get that what she's doing right now to me is that exact thing? "You will tire of my issues, and then where will that leave me?" That tears right through me. "I can't do this, Cameron."

"I thought you knew me better than that," I say, and I can see it in the way her body is reacting to me this is killing her as much as it's killing me. "Fate, I can see in your fucking eyes you don't want to end this, so why are you doing this?" Her eyes go cold. The Fate I have known vanishes before me.

"Because I'm better off alone."

Breathing is the only thing keeping me alive.

Chapter Seventeen

Fate

UTTER DARKNESS. THAT IS where I am. And I deserve it. As I sit in the middle of the room, the fear is destroying my body from the inside out. This is the chaos I must intentionally put myself through so that it takes away from my other pain. The panic is crippling. However, this agony takes the sting away. It's a distraction from my true pain. In the distance, someone's calling, but I try to pull myself further down into my personal hell.

"What are you doing?" Clarissa screams, but I barely hear her. I'm gone. Fate is no longer here to care.

"Where is Cameron?" It's barely a whisper in my mind, but his name continues to ring through. My mind begins to torment me.

He will think you're damaged. Dirty and used up, broken beyond repair. Why would he want that when he can have a perfect person who can give him everything he needs? Why would he want Fate? Push him away. Send him running. Do you want him to see you the way others who know about you have?

"I sent him away. It's done. We are done," I choke out the words and try to think back to my nightmares because they are less painful than this. The burning wipes out everything else.

"Why would you do that?" she croaks and I don't need to peek at her to know she's crying. No, I can't take it anymore. Deeper I go to find the fire to burn it all away.

"Tears, I like it when you do that. Fear me, it makes you know your place." His hands are unsteady and his words slurred.

"Fate," she screams.

"Because he will find out, and you're right, it's not a good idea," I say softly as I bring myself back into my hell. *Music. Darkness. Touching.*

"And this is? Sitting in the dark traumatizing yourself is the answer?" Clarissa wails, and I can barely see her anymore.

My world is shutting down, and I'm at peace in my strange surroundings. Like I'm untouchable. I welcome the pain, I know this pain and where it leads.

"It takes away the pain," I respond deadpan.

"Get up," Clarissa demands.

I don't respond. I continue to let myself go further and further inside. Away from this devastation and to where the pain is from those nights. The only pain that can eliminate the one I fear. The memories that destroy my body and soul, tainted and ruined for the world. No turning back. My body craves this. The pain I have lived with, the only fears that I can stomach above this earth-shattering abyss. Further I go. Opening those childhood memories and the nights where the monsters weren't coming from under my bed, but from the door that led to the hallway. A time in which I felt like I'd never survive but was able to continue. Only just breathing, that was my life. Now I can barely do that. Deeper into those nights; away from the pain of living without Cameron. Into my nightmares where he haunts me, where he always finds me. A place that makes it easier to breath.

He locks the door, and the click is deafening. He's not going to leave me alone. I will never be free. Always coming. Never letting me go. I deserve this. I made him mad. You shouldn't make him mad. I didn't mean to say anything. I was sad and it came out.

My mind dives in deeper and I lose myself into a place I fought so long to stay out of. There's nothing, but best of all, I feel nothing. The emptiness is freedom.

The evil in his eyes, the panic in my body, and then shear fear of the life I have to live. Take me there. Anywhere but here, where I'm everything he told me I was. Dirty, tainted, unlovable.

"Fate."

My eyes blink open, and I struggle to focus, still groggy.

"You're fine, you've just been resting," a woman says, and I glance around frantically. "You need to stay calm."

That only makes my panic escalate. Where am I? Where is Cameron? Just like that, the wave of pain of everything I've done comes back. "Cameron," I whimper.

"It's okay."

Clarissa is standing by the door with a man I assume is a doctor by his clothing. The room reeks of the one smell I hate more than that of my birth father. I'm in a hospital.

"They are here to help you, honey. We all just want you better," she says and it all falls into place.

Staring at the walls, the smell and, most of all, the noises that come along with a place like this, it hits me. How could she do this to me? She was supposed to protect me and take care of me. "You had me committed!" I scream at her.

Clarissa flinches, and I become enraged. "Fate, you weren't responding, I didn't know what to do."

"I'll tell you what you don't do. Commit the person."

"You only have to stay for seventy-two hours."

"Get her out of here. I don't want her here. Get out," I yell, and the nurse takes Clarissa away with tears falling down her face. Another nurse comes in and she has a needle. Screaming out, I'm getting weaker as it takes effect. "How could you?" I keep screaming as I go deeper and deeper. "I will never forgive you," I call out as my body finally gives in to the drugs.

When I come to again, I'm alone in my hospital room. I try to move, but I'm in restraints. A nurse comes in as she must have heard me or was watching close by. "Fate, do you know where you are?"

The memories flood in but this time it's not the same. I'm full of regret and fear, but it's manageable. "What have I done?" I cry out softly, and the nurse checks me over before removing the straps from my hands.

"If you get upset again I'll have to put these on," she warns, and I'm foolish. I'm not in control here.

"I won't. I'm sorry," I say, trying to remain calm. "It was just too much and I couldn't…"

She comes to the bedside, lowering the rail and I'm a bit freer. "Clarissa explained what had happened to send you into your attack."

Attack? I guess that could be a name for it. I felt as if I inflicted it on myself to help take away the pain of everything else going on.

"She also said there was a young man. Do you want us to call him?"

"No," I blurt out. "Sorry, no, I...I think I broke up with him. He doesn't need to know I'm a complete psycho to top it off."

She shoots me a glare but doesn't say anything. "Well, you will have to stay here until your time is up. Then it is up to you what you want to do," she says, then tells me the psychologist will be in to see me shortly.

When the older woman walks in, I sense I'm never going to get out of here. The way she is watching my every move, I worry if I make the wrong one they will lock me up and throw away the key. She sits and tells me all about my care that has been going on while I was unable to care for myself. Clarissa is still here but can't come in unless I say so. She tells me about all my options, but honestly, I'm just not ready to think about it yet. I need to get out of here and breathe. It's as if I'm suffocating.

Finally, I say what I should have said when I first woke up. "Clarissa can make the choices." She gives me an odd glance but doesn't say anything else about it.

"I'll send her in," she finally says when she feels she's gotten enough from me. When Clarissa walks in, my guilt is agonizing. With dark circles under red-rimmed eyes, she appears not to have slept in days, as if someone took away all her coffee, leaving her unable to survive.

"I'm sorry I was so hateful," I say, unable to look her in the face. Clarissa is sniffling, and I know I'm to blame for all this. She doesn't deserve any of it.

"Don't you ever do that to me again, Fate. Do you have any idea how scared I was for you? I don't care if you hate me. You weren't functioning. What was I supposed to do, wait it out? What if you didn't get better?" she rushes out and then takes a deep breath. "Sorry," she says, giving me a small smile that doesn't quite reach her eyes. I've done this. Worn her down to where she has to put on a face to placate me.

"You did what anyone would, Clarissa. I wouldn't have come out of that by myself. I was purposely pulling myself into the pain to get away from the pain of losing Cameron." My mind drifts to everything I said. It was overwhelming to think of all the possibilities of him finding out and seeing me as repulsive. That would be the death of me. I know I have to tell him, and I will, but when I sense I've finally dealt with it. That way I can console him too, because if he doesn't run away from me, from my secret, it will break him.

"It's not over," she says, and my heart picks up a bit. "That young man has been calling me the whole time. I've run out of excuses. You were due back at the apartment. I had to tell him you weren't ready to leave home and would be back there soon. If that's what you want to do, Fate. I can't tell you what to do, but whatever it is you do decide, it has to be about what you want."

"Cameron," I whisper, and I know I've made the biggest mistake of my life.

"So, go back to school and be with him," she says it as if it would be so simple.

I can't just walk back into his world and throw all this at him. Not after what I've said. "I told him things

I can't take back, Clarissa. How can he ever forgive me for that? Now *he's* getting out too. My past is haunting me. I just want to be normal."

Clarissa lightly wraps her arms around me, as though she's trying to console me.

"Clarissa, what am I going to do?"

Chapter Eighteen

Cameron

"You can't just calm the hell down, can you?" Cecilia says, and I give her a screw you glare. Seriously, calm down? Fate has been gone for twelve damn days. Twelve. Clarissa told me she's fine and she texts me saying everything is fine, but no matter what she says, when Fate gets here, shit is still going to be all screwed up with us. "She's coming home any minute. You should be happy, not like you're about to keel over. Sit the hell down before you have a heart attack."

"Wait, you spoke to her?" I yell at Cecilia. Clarissa let me know to expect her, but not when.

She gives me a glance that says busted. "What the hell, Cecilia? You're my friend, why would you not tell me you talked to her?"

"Doesn't work that way. I'm her friend too," she says plainly, and I want to hit something.

"Do you know where she's been? Is she okay? Are we okay?" I say, and yeah, I know I'm pathetic, but I've been going out of my mind without her here. If I were honest, I wouldn't care as long as I could set eyes on her and make sure she's better. Seeing her that way was damn torture.

"Sorry, Romeo, you aren't getting anything from me. What she wants you to know, she can tell you. Your dumb ass should have listened to Clarissa when she warned you to just leave."

Yeah, like I haven't been saying that to myself since the moment I was out of that house. I should have listened, but I just didn't think she could be that bad. Even knowing what I know now, I'd still go in there to try to help her. "Just tell me she's okay," I beg.

"I'm okay."

I jump and turn around, coming face to face with the one person I need in this moment. She seems more herself than she was that day, but I still see there is strain. I have to put my hands in my pockets to keep them from reaching out to her. My mind is telling me I only get this one chance to do this right, and, for the sake of my sanity, I need to, because a world without Fate isn't something I could handle.

"Well, I kept him as calm as I could, but this boy is in need of a serious tranquilizer." Cecilia's mouth pops open, and she looks like she can't believe what she's said. *What the hell?* "I am so sorry. I shouldn't have said that. Wow, I'm so inconsiderate." Then she grimaces at me and can see my confusion. "Shit."

"It's fine, Cecilia," Fate says, and I have no damn idea what is going on, but I'm going to need some answers. Not all of them, but at least why Cecilia just went ten shades paler.

"Okay, I'm gone before I screw up any more." She waves and walks out the door without glancing back at the awkwardness she leaves behind.

Fate just continues to stand there, and all I can do is

watch. I'm scared that with any slight movement I will scare her off. "I should have knocked," she blurts out.

"This is your home." She needs to get her facts straight because I'm two seconds away from kicking her beautiful ass around our apartment. Now her eyes seem like they are unable to stare into mine. *Fuck.* I'm such an idiot. I never thought that maybe she was back for just school and not me. Shit, is she even back to stay? "Unless you're not staying." The words barely come out. I don't know what I'll do if she says she's just here for her stuff.

"I don't have to." Her eyes glance at the floor and it's like all those months of progress went out the window, taking my *Fate* with them. Without Fate here I can't stay. I might as well be the one to leave. At least I have other means to live somewhere else.

"If you don't want to be around me, I'll be the one to leave. I can't ask you to give up the semester because this isn't what you want or have you pay more money to live somewhere else. If you want to stay, I'll leave."

Her eyes snap up and gaze right at me. "What are you talking about, Cameron?"

God, it sounds so good to hear her say my name, even if it's only for now. "You don't want this, I get that. I can leave, it's only right. I pursued you. You didn't ask for any of this." She puts her bag down on the table and just walks into her bedroom, closing the door behind her. Well, that's what I guessed. Turning around, I go to my room to get some shit together. *I won't hurt you anymore.* If that's why she appeared the way she did in Orlando, I won't do that to her again. I will do whatever it takes to make sure she's never in that much pain again, even if it means having to endure that pain myself by walking away. My door creaks, and I turn around. There is Fate in the kitty pajamas from the day I met her. That wrecks me.

"What are you doing?" she asks and the hurt in her voice is like someone just stabbed her with a knife. "Oh." She turns, but I instinctively grab her hand. When she turns back, I immediately let go and wait for her to continue. "I won't be in your way. I don't blame you for leaving, I was horrible to you. Unforgiveable actually. I wouldn't want to be around me either."

"What? Okay, wait a fucking second. I think we are so screwed up that we don't know what the hell is happening." My mind is all confused, so I just have to be blunt and let the cards fall where they may.

"Got that right," she says and almost laughs. My whole body jumps at that. She's still in there. My Fate.

"I was packing some shit to go stay with Scott because I thought you wanted me to leave. That you didn't want this."

"I don't," she says, and I'm done. This girl just pulled the plug on me. She must notice because she starts talking again. "No. I mean, I don't want you to leave," she corrects, and it's like I can breathe again.

"You don't?" She shakes her head, and this charge builds between us. Something has happened here. "What do you want?"

"You."

I don't even think. I just do. I'm tired of over thinking this crap. I just need to show her. She needs to feel this. All of it. That way there isn't a question in that stubborn head of hers. I react the way my body has been begging me to since I saw her in these same fricking pajamas. I grab her and push her hard against the wall. We crash against it and she gasps. I don't stop. My mouth crashes down on hers, and she moans. *Damn.* I slide my hands slowly up her arms, and she doesn't pull away. She's meeting me step for step. Not missing a single one.

When she opens her mouth slightly, I go in and deepen the kiss. Her hands grip my shirt as I continue with her still pressed up against the wall. Then she surprises me. She puts her arms around my shoulders and wraps her legs around my middle. My hands find her waist and I grip her tightly. I. Am. Never. Letting. Go.

Home. That's all I'm sensing right now, and I'm not talking about the apartment. This girl is my home. There will never be another one like her. There is no return for me from this. I'm all in, and I hope to God she is too. When she starts pulling on my shirt, I know I have to stop this. I can't pressure her. We need to keep with what was working because if I go too fast and she bails, that's it for me. Game over.

"Does that clear things up for you?" I say breathlessly against her bare shoulder where my head is now resting. She lets go of my waist with her legs, and I pull back to let some air get between us.

"You don't hate me?"

Is this girl serious? "You are it for me, Fate. Stop pushing me away, because I'm not going anywhere," I say without thinking. I just laid it all out there for her to see. I showed her and now I've said it. Might as well go in for the kill. "I love you, so just let me in, for fuck's sake." Her mouth drops open in surprise and I love it. "Where were you, Fate?" I ask, and she shakes her head like she just isn't sure what to say. "Why didn't you come home? All this time could have been spared. Please talk to me," I beg her because I need something. Anything at this point is better than the unknown. The unknown has been what was screwing with my mind for the last eight days.

"I'm just nervous to talk about it." She takes a deep breath, and I finally get a glimpse behind those walls. "After you left I went to a bad place. I couldn't deal with the pain, and Clarissa had no choice." She is watching me so closely it's like I'm the one who is nervous.

"Where have you been, Fate?" Her face is full of apprehension. Does this girl not understand that she could tell me anything and it wouldn't matter?

"A mental hospital."

My mouth drops open. That I was not expecting.

Chapter Nineteen

Fate

WHEN I WALKED IN, he didn't even notice. Cameron couldn't get past that she would keep my confidence and not tell him about my inner demons. Once I spoke and he turned around, it was like in that moment, I knew. I would never be okay again if I couldn't repair the damage I'd done to this man. He's disheveled to the point I almost don't recognize the man before me, and he's a freaking rock star. He was still hot as hell and anyone would want to jump his bones, but he just didn't seem as if he cared about anything. I had to change because I felt as if my own clothes were suffocating me, and since I had worn them on the plane, I was completely uncomfortable. I needed to get into something familiar so I could have a very difficult conversation with him.

Coming into his room and seeing him packing a bag crushed me. I thought, in that moment, that I'd lost every chance of making him forgive me. Then, out of nowhere, he took hold of me and pushed me against the wall. I wasn't scared. I didn't flinch at the contact. I welcomed it. I know he'd never hurt me. When he kissed me, I felt like my world wasn't flat anymore. Lately, I'd been feeling like my world had been crushed, and, in that moment, he put it all back together. I knew it might be short-lived because we hadn't talked, but a girl needs things to dream about.

Then he asked me where I'd been and everything came crashing down again. I had to come clean. I might not be able to tell him every detail of my issues, but this I could tell him. He deserved to know what he was getting into if he forgave me.

"A mental hospital."

Cameron's face is one filled with shock. I want to pull away from him but his touch is keeping me grounded. He doesn't glance away. He just watches, and the pressure builds. Clarissa and I talked about this before I left, but saying it was a completely different thing. They let me leave the hospital, and Clarissa asked me to go into counseling here at the first sign of any issues. She also demanded that someone here know about my issues before putting me on a plane. That's where Cecilia came in. I wasn't sure she wouldn't go to Cameron, but I thought we were friends too. I told her I would tell him. Asking her to lie was not part of the deal.

"Cameron," I say, because I don't want to continue if this sealed things for him. Taking a deep breath and committing the feeling of his touch to memory for later, I step out of his grasp. "You can walk away now, I won't hold it against you, I promise."

"Stop."

I'm not sure if he means the talking or that I was pulling away. I'm silently praying it is the latter. To be sure, I just don't do anything. I'm completely still, waiting for him to give me some clue as to what he actually wants.

"Do you not realize how much I care about you?"

I just shake my head trying not to let him get a glimpse of me. Not because I don't know, but because he shouldn't. I can't say it back; it's a tainted word for me. The other part of me also worries that it's changed because he found out who I really am.

"Look at me," he commands, and I do as he says. His eyes tear right through me. "Fate, stop pushing me away because you think I'm going to leave. You could tell me anything, and it wouldn't change how I feel about you. When you love someone, all this other shit is just something to work through. They aren't game changers."

That night in my bedroom in Orlando he said he thought I knew him better than that. I think I'm finally starting to see that as much as I hide, he still sees it all. But the best part is that he doesn't care. It's unconditional.

"What happened?"

Truth time. "You know that I was hurt by someone."

He nods, and I'm happy he seems to just want to let me say this and get it over with.

"Well, he is getting out on parole. I only found out after being home for two days. It's why I pulled away. I couldn't deal with all my emotions. Unfortunately, even the good ones, and that meant you. Then you showed up and I was just so haunted by everything, I pushed you. It was something I couldn't control. I just kept telling myself you'd eventually leave anyway."

"I shouldn't have left. You needed me, and I walked out on you."

Oh, this was not what I wanted him to feel. "Please know that this was not your fault. Whether you stayed or not, it wouldn't have mattered. The only thing that would have changed is you would have had the same guilt as Clarissa when she took me to the hospital." Clarissa still struggles with what she did. I know why she had to, but that doesn't take her guilt away. Cameron wouldn't have been able to handle that.

"So that's why you didn't come home? You were there the whole time," he asks.

I take a deep breath; I'm about to show him more of my feelings than I ever have before.

"Actually, no. I was able to leave, and I went back to the house with Clarissa. I couldn't come back here. Not with how we left things. Not when I wasn't sure of what I was coming back to. The possibilities my mind went through just at the thought of your reactions are what kept me away." His hand rests against my check, and I lean into the warmth. I missed this. I missed all of him. The peacefulness I have by being touched by him is unlike anything I've felt before.

"What possibilities?" he asks as he grazes my skin with his fingers. Now he's just making it hard for me to think at all.

"Ah...well, I wasn't sure what I was coming back to. Did you want me to leave? Would you be okay with still being my friend?"

"We were never just friends, Fate," he states, and on every level I know he's right. From the moment he walked into my world, I knew. I fought it because I knew it would lead to some tough moments, but I know if he's by my side I can handle them all.

"No. So that was another fear. I didn't know if that

left anything at all. I was awful to you, and to just walk back in wasn't something I was looking forward to doing. I kept putting it off, and then Cecilia told me I had to come. I assumed maybe you wanted me to leave, so I came, but I was hoping it was because you've been as miserable as I have been. Cameron, I have never been as unhappy as I was without you in my life. I don't know what the future holds, but we can have our days. Each one of them endless to us, if that makes sense."

"Forever in a day," he says, and those words hit home with me. That's exactly what I was talking about. This man gets me. "So when you thought about coming back here to see me, what did you want to happen?"

"I wanted you to stay with me. Because as much as I hate to say it, I need you," I say truthfully, and a smile sweeps across his face.

"I need you too," he says and softly kisses me. "I felt all those worries too, Fate. When you're feeling something, tell me. It's the only way we can stay on the same page. I know you have limitations, and I won't push those. When you're ready, you will tell me whatever it is you're keeping from me. If that day never comes, that's okay too."

"Thank you." Knowing I don't have to tell him my story brings me peace. I know I'll have to talk to him about it one day, but today I can just be happy with Cameron.

"I have a question. How would this affect our baby steps? I'm not asking because I'm pressuring you to make new ones, I'm asking so I don't do old ones that would now bring you stress."

Of course Cameron would think of our baby steps

and all that these new issues could come with them. "Here, alone. Nothing needs to change. But in public, I need to go back to where I was. I'm just not sure how I'd feel. I'm not saying no. I'm saying I'm not sure." Instantly, I flinch at the thought of him saying we are finished. I know it's unfair of me to even ask him to adjust to this way of life. To take a normal relationship away from him. "Cameron, I might never be able to do certain things. You may want to really think if this is what you want. Someone else with fewer problems may be suited better to your life. I can't promise anything but what you have before you. You deserve so much more than me." Being so honest about my fears and my thoughts is new to me. I always hide them, and it's time I just put myself out there. I don't want a life of 'what ifs,' I want a full life, even if it has some heartache. It will be worth it. Cameron is worth that risk.

"No. My answer is no," he commands, and my heart stops.

I'm unsure what he means, so I do what he's asked. I ask him. "So what are you saying, Cameron? Put me on the same page," I say, and he gives me that smirk I've been missing from my life for far too long.

"Nothing changed for me. No one can take your place, Fate. Shit, if anything, I love you more than I did before. You let me."

Chapter Twenty

Cameron

LIFE WITH FATE HAS been going so well since she came back. So, of course, something has to screw with that. In walks Trisha. "What the hell is she doing here?" I say to Scott and Cecilia. They just shake their heads, telling me they don't know shit either. Thank God Fate just went through the back door to the bathroom.

I brought Fate here today to see the practice space and get her comfortable. I know she's not ready to hear the music of the full band yet, but I think that day will come. We've moved past the earplugs when I play my guitar. I haven't plugged it into the amp or played my electric so there really isn't any more noise, but we are making progress. She has come so far since she got back, and I'm falling more in love with this girl every day. It's pathetic, but I wouldn't change it.

"Trisha, what the hell are you doing here?" This is the last thing I need right now. "You shouldn't be here. Fate is here, and we both know it will do no one any good to have you here." Fate hates this girl, and with good reason. I can't say I'd be okay with one of her exes sniffing around if she had one. We've talked about relationships, but she hasn't been in one. I love that more than anything. Having Trisha show up here just screws with everything in my life. I don't want her here. This girl is trouble, even I hate when she's around.

"I wanted to see my baby," she says with a little pout. This has always been her game. I used to play to get a piece, but that's just not happening anymore.

"I'm not your baby. I never was. Besides that, I told you, I'm with Fate." I drag out her name, hoping she gets the hint.

"But you're not exclusive, so here I am and we should go. I've missed you so much. Let me show you what you've been missing," she says with a smirk, trying to be sexy. It's not working. Only one thing does it for me. *Fate.*

"What the hell do you mean, not exclusive?"

"I don't blame you for not doing this because I wouldn't want to be tied to her either." I give her a glance like 'what in the hell are you talking about.' "Well, you guys haven't come out, so I take it she isn't your girlfriend. I don't mind sharing." Her words make me want to bend over and puke. Going there with her again just isn't going to happen, and God help me if Fate decided to fall for someone else.

"What do you say, Cam?" Her calling me Cam only reminds me of that day when Fate told me about never calling me Cam. To her it sounded dirty. I can't blame her, I made it that way, and hearing Trisha say it now just makes that feeling more damn real.

"What I have to say you won't like, Trisha. We aren't going public because that doesn't matter to us and she's not ready. Not because I don't want to be tied to her. I'd lock myself to her and throw away the only key. Do you get what I'm saying? You aren't getting back with me, with or without Fate. Our time, if we ever had one, is over." Where the hell is Fate? I glance at Cecilia, who just puts her hands up to say she doesn't know.

"She's just some girl," Trisha yells as I leave in search of Fate.

Walking through the back door to the bathroom, I immediately halt.

"I told you she wasn't anything special," Trisha says quietly from behind me. I didn't know she had followed me, and I can't believe what I'm seeing. They haven't seen us yet, but my heart is beating so hard as if it's going to crash through my chest.

"Oh, come on, sweetheart, you're not into him, so why worry what he thinks, right?" Dex, another member of the band, says and I want to go to her, but Trisha holds me. Almost as if she's telling me to watch. "If you really were just interested in him you'd be telling the whole world." His arms are a cage around her against the wall and she appears like she is in a panic. He starts to bring his hand up to her shoulder, which is bare from her shirt falling off to the side.

"Please. Don't. Touch. Me," she says as she is fighting back tears. Just as he goes to put the tip of his fingers on her, she screams. "I said don't touch me." She pushes him, but he quickly has her back in the cage of his arms. I've seen enough.

"What the hell? Get off her," I shout, and I startle both of them. Dex peeks at Trisha, and I follow his eyes. She has the biggest smirk on her face.

"Cameron, man, I didn't see you there. Sorry to keep the band waiting," he says slyly.

"No, I mean what the hell are you doing touching

her?" I start to walk up to them, and he moves, putting some distance between them. Glancing at Fate, she is struggling to keep her breath steady.

"She wanted it. She's just worried you're going to be pissed off that she's hooking up with other band members. You know, roommate code or some garbage like that."

Scott and Cecilia know about my feelings for Fate, but Dex is new to the band. He must just think we aren't together because we aren't publicly affectionate. Seeing Fate so exposed is like I can see right into her. She doesn't want me to out us right now. I'm sure because it would only bring more attention to her. So I play it safe. I keep it vague. "I highly doubt that. I live with her and I can barely even touch her, so she's not going to let some random do it. Get the fuck off her and apologize."

"No, it's okay. It's my fault. I'm just a freak," she whispers, but we all hear her and those words break me wide open. She has enough without this bullshit.

"It's okay, baby, I'm all about getting down with freaks too." His words are filthy. No one should be talked to that way, and definitely not Fate. He places his hand on her hip, yanking her to him, and I can't take it anymore. Something inside me snaps. I lunge for him, but Trisha gets in between us and pulls me back.

Cecilia and Scott come running in and stop when they see what's going on. Watching everyone, they are all stunned with the scene that is in front of us. Dex still has his hands on Fate, and she is just shaking her head. No one is saying anything, and then all hell breaks loose.

"Choose," Fate whispers and I break. I'm pulling Dex away, pounding my fists into his face as I get him farther away from my girl. Scott doesn't take long to pull me off him, and I peer around frantically, trying to see where Fate is. I quickly find her with her back in the corner of the wall with Cecilia trying to comfort her without touching her.

"Why the hell would you bring a banger chick around who doesn't want to be touched, man?" Dex says, holding his lip that is bleeding from my attack.

"She's not yours to touch." Walking toward Fate, I stop when Dex gets in front of me. "Getting between me and mine isn't a smart idea right now, Dex," I warn. "She isn't a banger chick or a groupie, so back the hell off before I beat the ever loving shit out of your sorry ass."

My words only seem to fuel him. He takes a step back toward Fate again, and she tries to pull herself farther into the corner away from him. His face tells me he enjoys that he's having this effect on her, and that makes me sick. "Nah, man, I think she wants it. She's not saying no, now, is she?"

Fate is scared into silence, and I know she must be screaming on the inside. The fear coming off her is paralyzing, as I'm sure Dex can tell, and he seems to be getting off on it. Unlike him, it makes me want to puke, but he seems to be more turned on by this shit. Sick bastard.

"Dex, you're asking for a beat down, man. Leave Fate alone," Scott pleads.

But Dex just laughs and goes to touch her again. Cecilia beats me to it and slaps him.

"All these chicks are feisty," he spits out, holding

his face. This gives Fate the chance to run out from the corner and she does. Straight into my damn arms, and she's breathing heavily against my chest.

"Oh, see how she plays the part so well. Can't you see through her games, Cam? I thought you were a better player than this."

Cecilia takes a step toward Trisha, but Scott grabs her, holding her back. "He may not see your shit, but I sure do Trisha. I was so happy the day he tossed your ass aside. You just can't stand it that he's happy with Fate since you never saw that with you. It was a drunken rock star, that's all you got. So take what you had and beat it, bitch, before I do that last part for you."

Trisha's face falls for a moment, but she quickly puts her game face back on.

"Let me guess, you told Dex she was just playing hard to get. You do this every time he brings someone new around. Trying to cut out the competition. Cameron has something catch his eyes and you get one of the guys that follow you around to go in for the kill, right? Because you know once Cameron finds out she's screwing with others, he's done. I don't know how you kept your sex with Dex a secret, but I didn't say anything about it since he tossed your ass to the curb like the trash you are. So, I spared him the pain, but you think I'm going to let you come in here and screw with Fate? You better think twice, Trisha. Unlike you, Fate isn't after a rock star, she's after Cameron. Something you've never had."

Glancing between Trisha and Dex, I don't even have to ask to know it's true they were screwing behind my back. With Fate here in my arms there is nothing else in the world that matters. I don't care what she's done or who she's done it with.

"Baby, it was just once and I regretted it right away. I didn't tell you because it didn't mean anything and I didn't want it to come between us," Trisha pleads.

"What the hell are you saying, Trisha? You came on to me, made me go after Fate to make him jealous and screw up again so we could boot him. Why are you messing with the plan now?" Dex says with confusion. Damn, he's an idiot.

"You thought we would kick the lead singer out of the band?" Scott says when he clues into this shit storm.

"I want them both out. If I have to see their faces again, we are going to have a problem. If that's a problem, I'm done with all this. I'll just take Fate and leave." Trisha is already starting her pleading, but I shut her out. Dex is yelling and Scott is just shaking his head in frustration.

"Trisha, shut it. You don't get it. I don't even care that you were with him. That should tell you how done I really am with you. All I care about is getting my girl back to our place, our home, so I can try to undo all this bullshit."

Fate's arms tighten around my waist, and I know how hard this touching must be for her with everyone watching. Especially after everything she's gone through lately. She can't handle the thought that someone might perceive her a certain way or take our picture. My girl is just getting back on her feet again. For that reason, we've never been pressed up against each other this way except in our apartment. It's definitely not a baby step.

Chapter Twenty-One

Fate

FEELING HIM AGAINST ME isn't new, but doing so in front of others is. You'd think I'd be panicking, but I'm not. Something about Cameron is pulling me closer every time I touch him. It scares me, and it's as if I'm going to be consumed by him at any moment. That is the worst feeling. Not because I don't want that, it's because I do, and that makes me vulnerable. I know, I'm the one who puts this space between us, but now I'm questioning why. I'm done hiding my life with him.

Yelling pulls me from my thoughts, and all I can do is stand there in the safety of Cameron's arms, watching these events unfold.

"Scott, I'm serious. Either we find a new bassist, or you get yourself a new singer and guitarist," Cameron states firmly. "So what's it going to be? I have other shit to deal with."

Without a moment's pause, Scott speaks, "Dex, you're out. Maybe next time don't try to screw with the lead man's girl." Dex starts yelling, but none of them seem to care. Then one of the security guards comes and grabs Dex by the arm, leading him out.

"The skank too," Cecilia says, pointing to Trisha.

Turning, I give Cecilia a small smile and mouth, 'I owe you one.' She just winks at me.

"Baby, don't let them do this to us, I love you," she says, and I tighten my hold on him.

"He's mine," I whisper without meaning to say it aloud. *Crap.* He chuckles against me, and I know he's trying to rein it in.

Cameron leans down and whispers to me, "I am yours." His arms tighten around me, and it's like he's validating my fragile feelings.

Is he just doing this because he's trying to save me like she said? I can't help the doubt. Just because I'm trying to be better doesn't make those thoughts go away.

"Baby," he says jokingly to Trisha. "I'm not letting anyone do anything. There isn't a relationship between us to screw with. Time to go."

Peeking up at him, I notice he wasn't even looking at her the entire time. He was watching me. I take a chance. *Fate, do not fail me now.* Standing on the tips of my toes, I reach up while bringing my hands behind his head, pulling him down to close the space between us. I bring my mouth to his, and he gently returns the kiss. I barely hear Trisha still screaming in the back as I continue kissing him. His lips are soft against mine, like he's scared he's going to break me. Pulling him closer to me, I increase the intensity of the kiss and his hands rest against my backside. Having him hold me in any way is amazing. A cough and a whistle from behind us remind me that we are not alone. I don't turn around. Pulling away from him instead, I place my face in his chest, and he just chuckles.

"Well, shit, my girl has got some serious moves," Cecilia says, whistling at the end. "The wicked bitch is gone, and you just showed her who he belongs to. Trust me when I say he's never been as happy as he is right now." Leave it to Cecilia to only further embarrass me, because I'm sure that wasn't as amazing for him as it was for me.

"If you let this one go, you're a damn fool, you hear me, Cameron?" Scott says, and I wonder how he gets away with being so blunt with him when he doesn't usually let people tell him how to be.

His hand comes under my chin, bringing my face up so I'm staring into his eyes. "Don't I know it? Never going to happen," he says, and I just smile. "Well, time to get my girl home to bed," he says with a wink. Cecilia and Scott laugh behind me.

Playfully smacking him, I just laugh. "Keep dreaming, McAlister," I say, pushing away from him.

He grabs my waist and brings me against him, and I stop. The warmth of his body stirs desires in mine. "If you keep calling me McAlister, I won't have to dream, McKenzie." He's sexy and he knows it. He uses it against me often, so I turn the tables on him.

Sliding my finger down his chest, he shivers beneath my touch and that gives me the power to continue my tease. "Well, if you keep calling me McKenzie, we might just have to figure something out," I say, giving him a wink before I push away from him, walking over to the door. "Bye, guys." I wave to Cecilia and Scott, but I notice Cameron is frozen in the same spot I left him.

Cecilia bends over in a fit of laughter, and Scott just chuckles, shaking his head. That snaps Cameron out of it, and he just stares at me with so many questions in his eyes. "Damn, my girl, Fate, has better game than

Cameron. I never thought I'd see the day," Cecilia says when she finally stops laughing.

"Coming, Cameron?" I say.

"Almost." He shakes his head, and I hear him, but I don't think he intended for me to. This only has Scott and Cecilia to start laughing again. I wait for him to come to the door and hold my hand out for him to grab. He does without hesitation. He is quickly learning what I can and cannot handle. That's what makes him Cameron. We walk the whole way back to our apartment holding hands. When we get to the lobby, we still have people gawking at us, but a few have become used to seeing us this way.

Once inside, I tell him I'm going to get changed, and I go to my room. I want to try something tonight, but I'm not sure how it will work. We have been able to sleep on the couch together but never in a bed. It's my forbidden zone, but I'd like to change that. I know I'm not ready to invite him into mine. That would be too much, too soon. I put on a pair of pajama shorts and a tank top before I walk out of my room.

He's sitting on the couch waiting for me, wearing his usual pajama pants and a T-shirt. He could be in rags and he'd still be the most beautiful person in the world to me. Not because he's gorgeous, but because of his heart. His inner truth calls to me, making the beauty of this wonderful man bring out the destroyed beauty in me. He watches me approach.

"I'm like a moth to the flame when it comes to you, Cameron. I'm just praying I don't get burned," I say as I take my place next to him on the couch, waiting for him to say something.

"You act as if you're the only one who could be hurt

by this. Do you not realize I'm the one who's all in? I'm in a sea of fish, but they're all in black and white. You're the only fish that's in color, my beautiful girl." To many people his words wouldn't mean anything. But to me, this is everything. He understands me in every way: my struggles, my anxiety, and the crazy way I talk about things in relation to marine life.

"Why me? You're a freaking rock star. You could have anyone you want, girls far more your caliber than me." For some reason I just can't look at him. I put my hands in my lap and just watch them. One of his hands slides across, and he places it over mine.

"Fate. I know I don't know everything you've been through. If I never know the full extent of it, I'm fine with that. As long as I have you, whatever piece of you that you can give to me, I will damn well take," he says, and he uses his other hand to turn my face toward him. "You are like nothing I've ever seen before. You give me hope in a world that had become so dark to me. You are my light. Nothing makes me feel more complete than you letting me get you through this darkness." His thumb slides across my bottom lip and I tremble. "Don't let my confidence fool you. I'm worried as shit that once you're ready to take the world on by yourself you won't need me and I'll lose my light and fall back into darkness. A world without Fate, well, that's just something I'm not interested in."

"I'm just as worried that once you put me back together again I'll be just another girl to you and you will go off to save the next girl," I say honestly.

"I thought I explained it pretty fucking well with the fish scenario," he says. "French Angel Fish," he states, and I give him a confused gaze. "That book you gave me to read, well, I did. They are monogamous and very territorial, that's you for me. You're my French Angel Fish. Fate is fate, and you're mine, babe," he says as he pushes a piece of my hair out of my face.

"I just got out-fished by a rock star," I say in complete awe of this man. "How can I argue with that?"

"You can't, babe, you can't stop fate. My fate is falling for you, and man, have I fallen."

His words make me panic, he knows my issues with certain words and he knows exactly how to keep me out of the red. That also scares the crap out of me because it means everything I'm feeling is real. I couldn't dream someone more perfect than him. All I do is ruin things and now his band has been my latest destruction. "I'm sorry you had to get rid of Dex because of me," I say to him, and I truly mean it. I don't know if I did something to mislead Dex, but I feel responsible for them having to find a new band member.

"Fate, Dex wasn't our first bassist, the next one might not even be our last. Scott and I started this band together and brought in a bassist and another guitarist when we needed them," he says to me, holding my shoulders, glancing into my eyes.

"Still."

"Fate, there are many things in life that are out of our control, and his actions are just one of them. This isn't the first issue we've had, but it will be the last one." His hand falls against my cheek, bringing an intense heat from his touch. "None of that matters. You matter. I keep worrying that one day I'm going to wake up to find that this is all just a dream. That I dreamed of this amazing girl who damn near wrecked me. That's the worst feeling. It's like waiting for the other shoe to drop. Sometimes I just can't shake it. But this..." he says, caressing my cheek. "This is my way to know it's real."

Gently, I place my hand over his. "I'm real and you're stuck with me until the end of the school year."

"I'm hoping forever," he says, and for once, I don't feel like that's impossible.

Chapter Twenty-Two

Fate

I continue to tug on the dress; Cameron just grabs my hands trying to distract me. His touch does that and now that he's caught on, he uses it. Especially when he can feel me stressing about things. Clarissa had come out for a few days during the Christmas holidays but had to leave yesterday on Christmas Eve. She had offered to work so some of the others with small children could stay home. Even on Christmas, she still has to go out and protect kids. It's sad that some holidays aren't filled with happiness.

So here I stand in front of Scott's parents' house, getting ready to meet the closest thing to parents that my boyfriend has. Yes, I've started using that term and I have to admit it's grown on me. I've put a stop to him not touching me in public. If we do it at home, he can do it out here. When we walk in, there is a cheer from the family who is sitting around in what seems to be the living room. It is enormous. Seriously, I think it's the size of Clarissa's entire main floor of her house, and it's just one room.

Before I know what is happening, I'm pulled from

Cameron and hugged tightly by a woman in her mid-fifties. I can see Cameron's face, and it has got panic written all over it. "Mom, I told you not to," Scott says, and his mom lets go immediately.

"Oh, I forgot. I am so sorry. I'm just so excited to finally meet you. The boys talk about you often, and, well, Cecilia is always going on about you as well. I just feel like I already know you. I'm sorry, dear." She is disturbed by her actions, but I can say I didn't flinch.

"Actually, it's okay," I say, and Cameron glares at me as if he doesn't believe me. "No, really, I'm not sure what they've said, but if Scott told you about touching, then you know enough. I've been working on it, and I'm doing much better," I say, and Cameron gives me an unsure smile. I mouth the word 'therapy' to him, and he nods. I've been seeing a victim's councilor here, and I have to say it's been so helpful. She's been teaching me it's not about the touch but the intent behind it that usually sets me off. When I'm unsure of the person, I panic without thinking. So, instead, I need to drill it into my head until they give me a reason to feel that way, to just kind of roll with it.

"Well then," Terry says as she comes in for another hug, and I close my eyes. It's nice to not have the panic issues. I'm not saying it will never happen again, but as long as I'm covered, and it's my hands only, I seem to be making great progress. Or so says my counselor, and she's the expert, right? When I open my eyes, Cameron is watching me with an expression of awe.

After introductions I find out that Scott's dad is named Lawrence. He's a shy man and he seems to keep to himself. Scott's mother is another story. From the hug, her love only continues as she dotes on me the entire time. Cameron just continues to sit back and watch with an odd expression on his face. The family tells stories, and I get to see a different side of Cameron. Here, he is carefree, and I usually only see that when he's with me at home. I like knowing that he has somewhere else he can be this way too.

After dinner, the family exchanges Christmas presents, and I'm shocked that they all thought to get me something. I haven't been around more than Clarissa for the last eight years and I find it overwhelming, but I sense the change within me too. Finally, I'm starting to feel whole again. Normal again, without an impending doom, and that is because of the strength Cameron gives me.

We finally make it back to the apartment and relax. I'm beginning to feel the stress of our first Christmas together. Did I make the right choice of a gift? Worst of all, I worry that he will hate it or not understand my sentiment. My mind is thinking of how this could be a moment for us. Special and new, moments to mask my nightmares. "Cameron, could we do this in your room?" I say, pointing to the gifts.

He gives me an odd, confused grin but nods his head.

I tell him I'm going to get in pajamas and meet him in there. Once I'm into my kitty pajamas that he adores so much, I make my way to his room. He's sitting in his desk chair, waiting for me. I climb onto his bed and make myself comfortable then pat the spot next to me.

He slowly approaches, making sure not to touch me, but he does sit next to me. "I was thinking, instead of the couch tonight, we could try sleeping in here. I'm sure that couch isn't doing wonders for your back." I try to joke because he just appears uncomfortable with what I just said.

"Fate," he says with a deep breath. "I'm fine where we are. I don't need to be in the bed. I just need to be with you," he says, and my soul ignites with affection for this man who continues to amaze me every day.

"I'm not. I need a baby step," I say with a pouty face, hoping it will work.

"What if you can't? What if you have nightmares?" he questions. Time to put it all out there for me.

"If I can't, I'll go back to the couch and I know you will follow. If I have a nightmare, I know that you are here with me to keep me safe. That no matter what, you won't let anything happen to me. As long as I have you, I think I can do that. You give me that. You take away those memories and fill them with ones of affection and trust. My boyfriend makes all that pain go away." The admiration in his eyes as I speak is enough, and I mean everything I say.

"How can I argue with all that?" he says coyly.

"You can't, now open your present," I say cheerfully, but then nerves sneak up. Handing him the box, I'm not sure about the gift now. When I had put them together, I was trying to think of what to give a person who has everything. So I did this. When he opens the box and sees them, his face turns to shock and I'm not sure what to take from that. *Is that a good sign?*

"Fate, when did you have time to do this?" he asks, and I know he's trying to think of times I snuck off. Honestly, the only time was when he was in class and I wasn't, or he was at band practice.

"I wanted to give you something that could hold your two passions," I say, using his words about being passionate about me and then music, in that order. So I made these. I designed six notebooks for only Cameron to use. On the front, I had Ten Ways Gone written in different dark colors everywhere with a picture of their stage set up behind it. When he opened them, he saw what I had written inside. There were also pictures of us on the inside at various times these last five months.

"Touched by Fate." He reads the words, and my heart stills.

"I thought you could use it to work on music. A piece of me that is with your music unconditionally."

"I was wrong. This was exactly what I needed and you knew it without me knowing. How do you do that? It's like you can see into me. You know when I need this." He touches my bare shoulder. "When I need this." He leans in, pressing his lips against mine. I'm finding it hard to break away every time we start this now. My body craves more. "But most of all this," he says as he slowly pulls his shirt off and exposes his chest.

"Oh my God." Peeking at him, I can't believe it. Bringing my fingers to his chest, I trace along the lines, and he shivers under my touch. "Cameron."

Gently, he places his hand over mine. "No Judgment, Only Fate." He reads the words that are tattooed on him, but the addition of 'Only Fate' brings tears streaming down my face. "I love you, Fate." His hand opens and a gold heart pendant is hanging from it.

I put my hand out to touch it and it turns, showing me the engraving. "Choose," I say, trying to stop the overwhelming feeling of his love that has come over me. I have to push back the negative feelings my body has but it's getting easier each time. He makes it easy to be with him. To *choose* him, I won't ever *choose* anyone else. In this moment it's everything people tell you about, when they know they've found that someone special. The trust, the joy, it's endless. "Cameron. I don't know what to say."

"You don't have to say anything. I know what you're feeling because I am too. Our life is just beginning, but now it's finally written somewhere. Where it belongs, right over my heart," he says, taking my hand in his and then placing it over his heart. "Now you can carry my heart and our word with you too." Some moments are those of a lifetime of emotions. This moment is one for me. "Because you have it, Fate. It's yours."

Chapter Twenty-Three

Fate

THE LAST MONTH HAS been a whirlwind. The holidays are done and getting back into school was a bit of a headache, but Cameron was in some of my classes and that made it easier. We have put a stop to everything when it comes to my hiding. It is hard, but I've started coming out of my shell and Cameron is the reason for that. He knows when to push and when to let it go. We only had one incident where things had a bump during that whole month. Someone from the media started digging around, and I had to argue with him to let it go. There were lots of things going on: the band had a new bassist, and the talk of a tour was now no longer just talk. It was happening. Trisha was trying to sway the media, saying they were together and such. He never refuted it, but I didn't need him too. I had him with me every night and I reminded him of that option.

Everything was returning to normal until we ran into Dex off campus. Luckily, I was able to distract Cameron. He was infuriated, but like he does for me, I was able to ground him. That control made me feel warm, as if it isn't just me who is consumed by the sheer need of him. He feels that too. However, from that moment, he was different, distant for some reason, and I felt disconnected to what had become my life support.

"What's wrong, Cameron?"

He doesn't say anything at first, and it seems like he's drifting. Moments between us play in my head.

"Tell me what you're feeling."

"I can only get in those walls if you let me."

Trying to live up to the promise I've made to be more transparent, I do as he's asked. "Something happened back there. I can't break through your walls either, you know, you're hiding. Like, you're pulling away from me for some reason, and that frightens me more than I'd care to admit," I say truthfully.

His whole demeanor changes and my old Cameron is back. "I'm sorry. I didn't mean to push you out of my head." My hand goes to his chest, and his hand finds my face. "I don't like when you see me that way," he says with such pain in his voice. "I worry that something might happen and you may be caught in the crossfire."

"You would never hurt me, Cameron. I know that. I wouldn't be where I am with you if I thought you could." This man doesn't trust himself very much, and that hurts my heart. Those actions with his mom have tainted him just like my past has done to me. "You can't save everyone," I say, because I think this is more than just about what he is saying.

He's obviously torn, but worse, he's defeated. "But I will save you."

"Cameron, I don't need you to save me. I need you

to be there for me. Help me, guide me, and care for me. It's not your job to save me." I don't ever want him to feel as if I'm this girl who needs a hero, even if it might be true. The guilt if something were to happen to us, or me, would eat at him.

"My job is to take care of you. Saving you included." His words are firm.

I know he doesn't want to argue, so I try a different approach. "Can't we save each other then?" As I gaze into his eyes, I know he is hearing my plea. At some point we need to do this together, and I'm hoping he will now see that I'm not as breakable as that girl he met on the first day.

"That sounds amazing, actually," he says, and I know I've won him over with my words, but he becomes serious again.

"Fate. I need you to promise me something."

"Anything," I say without thinking. Nothing comes to mind that I wouldn't be able to promise this man.

"If you ever find yourself in a situation with me like when I went after Dex, I need you to stay back."

My heart sinks because when this went down all I could think about was getting to him. "But if something like that happens, the only thing that makes it better is you."

"You have no fricking idea what that does to me. To know you are taking those damn walls down brick by brick, not just for you, but for me."

"You don't get lost in my darkness," I say truthfully, because he doesn't. Maybe because he doesn't know all the facts, but my history doesn't taint him the way it has others in my life.

"I will always find you," Cameron declares.

"I promise that I will not intentionally put myself in danger, but I won't make a promise I can't keep. When things like that happen, my body, my heart, goes to where it feels safe. That will always be you."

He is shocked by my response. "That's all I can ever ask of you. I can't say I don't understand, because nothing feels better in times of pure shit than having you in my arms." He pulls me to him and embraces me tightly. Moving my hair to the side with his finger, he bends down, whispering in my ear. "Sometimes my rage can blind me. Especially when it comes to someone hurting you. In that moment, stay back. Get Scott. Don't get close. I would never hurt you on purpose, but that doesn't mean the other person wouldn't. If something happened to you, I'd be done. There'd be no coming back for me. My fate would be over."

Tears fall from my eyes at his love. "Cameron, you really are too good to be true," I whisper back to him. "Never leave," I say, showing all my vulnerabilities.

"That will never happen, babe. I would have to be dead to be away from you, and even then I'd be with you." This man is far too beautiful for a girl like me. Not just physically. No one can ever tell me this man is not the most amazing person I have ever met. He always puts me above him. He is tender and takes joy in our baby steps. Thinking of a world without that is something I too could not handle.

"Don't say that. I can't think about something happening to you. It hurts my heart. We are just going to have a beautiful life, McAlister," I say, trying to lighten the mood.

"McKenzie, I know we will." Nothing sounds better than a life with Cameron.

We decide to get some studying in while we still have time. After an hour, I'm already over it. I can't absorb anything else. That happens sometimes when he is so close. Getting a glimpse at my phone, I remember. *Crap.* "Can I use your phone? Mine is dead and I forgot to call Clarissa," I ask because I know she's going to be upset. This isn't the first time our moments have led me to forget to call her. I can't help it. Cameron takes me away from this world. Into our own little one where I'm safe.

"Sure, it's in my room. I'm going to take a shower. Tell Clarissa I said hello and not to work so hard," he says jokingly, and I laugh too, telling him I will.

Clarissa isn't as annoyed as I thought she would be. She says she was out with friends, but I think she might have met someone and just doesn't want to tell me yet. I don't want her to be alone. She deserves to be happy and feel all of what I do with Cameron. She starts telling me she has found a new house that she has fallen in love with. "You will love it. I can't wait for you to see your room."

Peering around Cameron's room, it's like I'm in my room already. Sleeping in here with him has become a nightly routine for me. I've had no issues, and he's continuously telling me we can take back steps if we need to. That's not going to happen. I can't explain the happiness when I'm lying with him at night.

Something catches my eye; it's one of the notebooks I made him for Christmas sitting out. I can't help but turn the page and, when I do, my mouth drops open at all the scribbling of lyrics. They all surround one thing, though. Me. My name is written all over the page.

Fate took me down.
Now is her time to finally shine.
She broke in and opened my world
I can finally show the world what is mine
She gave me forever in a day
She takes all that darkness and pain away
Love isn't her word but she shows
I know come what may
All will be okay
Because of forever in a day

My heart stops. Clarissa is still talking, but I don't know what about. Written in front of me is a song. A song about me, about our *forever in a day*, something I thought were just words. Moments when he said things to make me feel better. Yet here they are, being written so he can share his thoughts with the world through his second passion. Showing them his ultimate one. I know the old saying is *forever and a day*, but what he's written is beautiful, our own personal piece that defines us as a whole.

"Clarissa. I have to go." I won't tell him I saw this, but I have this overwhelming urge to touch him, to be with him. No more holding back.

"Okay, honey, call me in a few days. I love you."

Clarissa is gone, and I go to hang up, but there is a message waiting and I accidentally open it while trying to disconnect the call. "Oh no." The message that just came through on Cameron's phone is from Trisha. It's a picture of her and she is wearing a see-through lingerie outfit with the words *see you soon* written under it. I'm going to puke.

Chapter Twenty-Four

Cameron

WHEN I WALK INTO my room and see her staring at the phone, I panic. She is as white as a ghost, and I'm scared something has happened to make her so fearful. When she sees me, she smiles but something is wrong with it. It's all fake and shit. Not like the Fate I get to see in our home. She's as real as I am, but the girl in front of me isn't just hiding. She's getting ready to run.

"What's going on?" I ask her, and she just shakes her head. Checking my room my notebook is lying there. Maybe that's what got to her. She saw something in there she wasn't ready to hear. But the way she continues to grimace to the phone it's as if I'm losing a battle I didn't even know I was in.

"I'm fine. Actually, I was thinking about going back to Orlando for the weekend," she says, and I can't even use my words. Why all of a sudden is she going to Orlando? "I just thought it'd be a good time with you having meetings about tour dates and I could see Clarissa." She's lying. I can see it right before my eyes.

"I can see you're sad even when you smile," I finally say, and she's startled. As if I've caught on.

She hands me my phone, walking away to her room and a message comes in. It's from Trisha, and I cringe. Glaring at it I'm in shock, she sent me a picture before and now she's asking me if I'm coming.

"This is what's going on." She turns to me and I'm right. She saw the picture.

"I don't talk to her. I haven't since the last time you saw her. This is her screwing with us, don't let her win." She hasn't contacted me and I didn't go trying to find her. She's nothing to me and Fate needs to see that. When it all comes down to it, I will do whatever I have to do to be with Fate. Only Fate. I don't feel like I'm giving anything up either. She's it for me. Trisha's picture does nothing for me. I'm nauseated at the hurt that I'm sure Fate is feeling.

"I'm not. I just want to go see Clarissa. Get away from this all." There we go, she let it slip at the end and I know I'm right.

"Away from me."

She shakes her head and tries to figure out what to say next. I don't want to give her the chance. I know I need to let her have some rope on this one. That way I can see how bad it really is. "Just some space. My head is spinning."

No, that's not going to help. Shit, it's worse than I thought. The last thing we need is all those damn miles between us. "Then talk about it," I beg, because I need her to. It's the only way to get over this mess my ex is bringing us right now. Note to self, I need to change my number first thing tomorrow. I don't need this happening again.

"When I get back we can." She leaves to go into her room to presumably pack a bag for her trip that I'm not sure she will come back from.

"Aren't you tired of running?" She's hurt, but I can't stop. "This is what you do, Fate. Shit gets tough. You have doubts and you bolt."

"I'm sorry for the way I am."

Oh hell, that's not what I wanted, but she needs to stop doing this because it's screwing with me too. I never know where I stand, and to some that might not be important, but she's my world. "Do you not care how much that hurts me that you wouldn't just come to me?" Why are we always coming back here? I thought we were past this, but it's like something keeps making her run. I think it has something to do with her past, but I know I can't bring that shit up or she will be gone forever.

"Of course I do, Cameron." She is just as hurt as I am now because I called into question her feelings for me. If that's what I have to do to get Fate back here to me, I will. "I just…you didn't go to the media to tell them you weren't with her. Maybe you're thinking why bother, you will just get back together anyway."

"No, it's because of you. If I went public and said I wasn't with Trisha they'd ask about someone else and they'd know. Any fool knows I'm in love." Her mouth drops open, and I think she finally sees the distance I will go for her. "I tried to shelter you from the media, but it just seems to backfire on me."

"Maybe this is just a sign it's not going to work. You're a rock star, and I'm just me. Maybe our worlds are too different."

What the hell! That sets me off. I can't believe she is saying this shit again. "It's like one step forward and two steps back with you, Fate." I never know if I'm making the right move here, but right now I know if I let her go to Orlando she's gone. "Only you can let me in. I can't push through those walls when you put them back up. Don't do this."

"I can't talk about this right now," she says softly.

"No matter what I do, you're always mad. Take a step back, you're mad. I say I love you, you're mad. I can't fucking win." She's scared by my aggressive tone, and I immediately regret the force behind my words. *Damn.* "Please don't leave, don't leave me." I walk up to her and cup her head in my hands, holding it in place so she can't look away. "Without your touch I'm not going to last, Fate."

Her eyes change. I'm not seeing the girl who was running. Fate is glancing back at me now. Those walls are letting me in for the moment, so I have to bring them down. "I tried to stay away from you, I just couldn't."

"I couldn't stay away from you either," she whispers, and I know I've gotten her back.

"I swear on my soul there is nothing going on between Trisha and me. Even if you weren't here, there still wouldn't be. I won't let her come between us. I promise you, Fate."

"So what do we do?" she asks, and I wish I knew. My phone beeps again, and Fate goes into my back pocket to grab it. It is another picture without the top piece this time. "Is she really that desperate?" Fate slips out, and I know she didn't mean to say it because she gasps in shock.

I can't help the laughter that comes from me.

"Wait, I have an idea," Fate says, and I'm worried and interested at the same time. She pulls me to our bed, in my bedroom. She pushes me against the bed, and I sit. She then yanks off my shirt, laughing the whole time like a fricking schoolgirl.

"I'm not sexting her back," I say in complete seriousness, because I'm not sure where she is going with that shit.

"Ya, that's not happening. Mine only, remember?"

Mine only. I like the sound of that. "That's right." Forever hers. I just wish she'd say that, but hopefully one day soon she will open up about whatever is weighing her down.

"Well, let's show her." If she wasn't Fate, I'd think this shit was about to become something that Scott was going to have to clean up later. She just seems so sure of herself. I can't help but smile. She turns and sits in my lap, making sure my tattoo is visible. Now I know what she's thinking. I wrap my free arm around her, making sure my tattoo is there for Trisha to see. She smiles in the camera, but I'm not even smiling. I'm just watching Fate.

She shows me the picture, and it's beautiful. She appears happy, and I look like I don't give a damn about anything but her. Her hand is right next to my tattoo. She captions it. *Pretty sure that says Fate. I'm busy coming with her.*

I burst out laughing. "Make sure I never let you go. I don't want to see that happiness with anyone but me." She squeezes me tightly and sends the picture. Trisha doesn't respond and I don't expect her to. Not much you can argue about when the girl's name is literally written on my heart.

We laugh about it for a good hour before I can tell she's getting tired. She falls asleep against me as I'm singing to her. It's become our newest baby step. I can't sleep, though, for some reason. The residency is loud tonight, and that might have something to do with it. I get up to leave so I can work on some lyrics and songs for the band. I don't want to do it in here in case I wake her. As I walk out the door, I glance back at her sleeping in our bed and there's a sting. This girl came out of nowhere. My life was nothing before she came around. Yeah, I was never alone physically, but until I met her, I didn't know what it meant to have someone. I don't ever want to go back to that empty feeling.

Out on the couch the noise has started to die down from the halls. I stop playing for a minute. Fate is whimpering. Quickly, I get up and run into the room.

"Please, no," she says aloud, and my damn heart breaks for this girl. Some sick bastard hurt her, and if I ever meet him, he will never touch a soul again.

"Fate," I say when I approach the bed, and she springs forward. I hadn't made it into the bed with her yet and she notices.

"You left me," she whispers.

"No, I just went out there to work on some music. You had a nightmare," I say, trying to calm her.

"No, in my nightmare. You left me."

That makes my body run cold. She had a nightmare about me leaving her. Not the bastard who has been haunting her for so long. "Fate, I don't care what happens. I'm not going to be the one to ever walk away from you. Do you hear me?" She nods, and I turn off most of the lights then climb into bed. She turns into me and snuggles up against me. Wrapping my hands around her, I know that no matter what happens, I will ruin myself and my happiness to spare her anymore pain.

Chapter Twenty-Five

Fate

"I need you not to freak out on me," Cameron says from my doorway.

I didn't even hear him come in, I was so deep in my studies. "Ya, that's not the way to start a conversation with someone," I say jokingly. "Nice try. Go away. I'm trying to study." I tease and smile at him.

"I'm not joking." He doesn't return my smile; my pulse spikes.

"What?" I whisper, feeling like he is about to pull the rug out from under me.

He walks over to where I sit on my bed, grabs my hand, and leads me into the living room. We haven't sat together on my bed much; it's my biggest trigger and he knows that. I sit down, and he bends down in front of me, placing his hands on my knees. I notice that there are papers sticking out of his pocket. When he sees my eyes on them, he pulls them out and lays them out in front of me.

Before me are several pictures of him and me together at various places. Even a picture of us kissing when we thought we were alone on a walk home one day. The headlines vary but they all are about us. '*The Fate of Our Rock Star*,' '*Can Fate Change a Bad Boy*,' '*Ten Ways Gone New Fate*,' they all surround me. The article has my full name in it, and panic makes my heart race. Apparently, sources told them the rock star has been spending his time with a new girl, the same girl. It goes on and on. The more I read, the more I'm overwhelmed. "Did Trisha do this?"

"I think so, but with the media you can never be sure," he says, and I can tell my reaction is hurting him. I'm sure most girls would be ecstatic for their name to be in print, but not me. This is something that I just didn't believe could happen. We are just college students. On some level, I know that's not all of it. He's a rock star with albums and multiple tours under his belt.

"We could go public," he says, and the blood drain from my face. My heart starts racing. That could bring some serious consequences for the things I'm trying to leave behind. I could just tell him why I don't want to, but the words don't come.

"Do we have to?" I say instead, and his face drop in disappointment.

He shakes his head and moves up to sit beside me. "We don't have to do anything you don't want to, Fate. It would just make them back off a bit if they got a story. Right now, they might keep going because it's a mystery to them."

I panic because lately I've been trying to tell him about my past. This, on top of that, will be too much for me. "How about we wait for now? Not too much longer. Let's wait until the end of the semester. That way we won't be in school if it gets to be a bother," I say, hoping he will go with that.

"If you think that's going to make this easier for you, of course. I just want the whole world to know that you are with me and I'm not the bad boy anymore," he says with a smirk, but I know he's serious about telling the world about us. I just don't want to do it until he knows the truth about me.

"You are the most amazing boyfriend, you know that, right?" The grin on my face is something I picked up from Cameron.

"I like when you call me boyfriend," he states with a huge smile on his face.

"Well, boyfriend, take me to practice," I say on a whim, and as soon as his face lights up, I know I said the right thing to get him out of this rut.

"Really? You want to come?" he says hopeful.

"Yes, I've seen you but never the whole band. I was thinking of coming with you more often. I enjoy listening to you, so I would love to." He bends down, kisses me, and lifts me up, spinning me around. The giggle that escapes me is carefree and it feels amazing. I don't know what I'd do without Cameron and my friends in my life now. They make the pain a little less every day and, when I'm with Cameron, I barely feel anything but his affection for me.

"You really do amaze me, Fate McKenzie. Thank you for coming out of that shell, for showing me how wonderful it is to be touched by fate." His words grip me. I can't believe he said my words for him back to me.

"Thank you for tearing down my walls. For everything you make me feel, Cameron. I don't think I'd be whole without you." He needs to know that when I say this I mean it, so I bring my mouth to his and kiss him. His touch means so much to me, and I love how far we've come with each other.

"You never have to find out," he says, and his tone is completely serious.

When we get to practice, Scott and the new guy are warming up. Once Scott sees me, he makes a cut motion to the bassist. "Hey, Fate, I didn't know you were coming," he says, but I know he's worried they won't be able to practice now that I'm here.

"I thought I'd come and listen to the band. I keep having to just listen to this one here and it gets to be a bit boring," I say jokingly, nudging Cameron. Scott smile is unsure as he glances at Cameron, who just kind of shrugs.

"Well then. This is Kent, he's our new bassist. Kent, this is Fate." He then turns his attention to Kent and has a warning expression. "Do not touch her or I will lose my damn mind. Cameron will also beat your ass."

Kent laughs and then glances at them as if he just got that it was a serious statement. "I don't think that's going to be a problem. My boyfriend isn't the sharing type." We all stop and stare at Kent.

"Well, he's a keeper," Cecilia says when she walks up behind me. "We don't have to worry about him, and I think I love his boyfriend already. I don't like to share either," she says with a smirk at Scott, who just shakes his head. Scott never cheats or strays an inch. He is all about Cecilia and he'd be stupid not to be. She is absolutely the most outgoing, affectionate person I have ever met.

"I don't share either," I say, giving both Cameron and Kent a grin. Kent breaks out in laughter and

Cameron is late to the game. He just stands there confused, and I watch it click.

"Oh." We all laugh at Cameron. He's always the joker, so a time like this is rare that he's the last one to clue in. "Well, I'm a rock god, who wouldn't want to share this?" he says in a cocky tone.

"And I'm Fate. I can judge your ass, remember that. It's written, so it must be true." Cecilia and Scott laugh at my comment. Cameron just stares at me as if I've grown another head.

"When did you get so funny?" Cameron asks.

"When I started dating a clown?" I say expressionless. The laughter coming from everyone else only fuels this moment. I can't help but join in.

"Rock star," he states.

"Hmm, well, get up there and show me what you can do then," I say in the most seductive tone I can. He blinks at me mindless for a minute. He turns away to go to the stage and I take a chance and smack his backside. "Definitely a rock god," I say with a smirk.

When he takes the stage, I get chills. The music starts and it's loud, but I'm safe. Cameron is in reach, and Cecilia is sitting here with me. My memories stay back and I keep my focus on Cameron. I can't tear my eyes away. He's incredible up there. His voice is something I'm used to hearing, but it never gets old. It calms me, same as his touch does. He could be singing the alphabet and I'd be in heaven.

After a few songs, they break, and Cameron comes up to me. "So, how was it?"

"Manageable. I handled it fine. Just something I'll have to get used to the same as the rest of it." I grin at him and watch his face turn up in a smile.

"How'd you like to watch us live in concert?" he asks, and I'm not sure what to say, but I go with the truth. It's the only thing that will work with my fears.

"I don't know if I could handle the crowd and being that far away from you, surrounded by people. It's you who makes this possible, Cameron. I'm not saying no. I just don't think I'll be there anytime soon."

"No, you wouldn't be in the crowd, you'd be backstage with Cecilia. Never alone and still close enough that I could see you. If it was too much you could just go back to the bus." Cameron stares at me, and I'm sure I could try. For him I'd try anything.

"That I could do, I think."

"How'd you like to come on tour with me this summer?" he says, and I know he's scared I'm going to say no. The thought of saying no actually scares me more because I've been dreading the thought of a summer away from him.

"Summer romance with a rock star sounds like an autobiography," I say with a smirk on my face. "I go where you go." And his face changes into one of complete love and affection.

"Fuck," he says and grabs me, kissing me without holding back. A summer of that sounds like exactly what we need.

Chapter Twenty-Six

Fate

"I WAS THINKING YOU could show me a bit about your world today," Cameron says, and I glance over at him clueless. Panic sets in when I think about having to tell him about my past and all that goes with that.

"What?" I mutter.

"I was wondering if, today, you would let me take you to the Aquarium."

That was not what I was expecting him to say. "You want to go to the aquarium? Why?" I ask.

"You're sitting here reading your books of facts and watching documentaries. I've read some of the books plus all the fun facts I learn from you. I figured maybe some hands on learning would bring my game up to where you are," he says in such a sweet tone that my heart jumps. "I know how you feel about the ocean, wildlife, and especially fish. Let me into your world, Miss McKenzie. Show me all the things you love about the world."

The word love burns into me. It's not something I use or like to hear because of the memories.

"Why are you doing this?" I beg him, and he puts his

hand on my bed beside me. I become frightened. I can't catch my breath, my world is spiraling out of control, and my heart beats in a frenzied, irregular rhythm. Not again, I pray.

"This is what love is." *His words haunt me. They always will.*

"Fate," Cameron says, pulling me from the past, and he puts his hand on my leg. It's like he's grounding me to the present and keeping my past where it belongs. His touch has a way of doing that for me.

"You really want to spend our day off from classes there?"

"I want to spend my day with you, and I want to see you in your happy place."

I don't know what comes over me, but I pull him to me. Placing my hands around his neck, I bring his lips to mine, and when he groans against my mouth, I deepen the kiss. Just as I go to pull away, I lightly nibble his bottom lip and his hands on my waist tighten. The power from this feels incredible. "You're my happy place," I whisper against his lips, and his mouth crashes down on me. Slowly, I lean back, and he has no choice but to follow me until my back is resting against the couch and he is holding himself up above me. He's careful not to put any weight on me or touch me other than with his lips. Before he can do anything to stop me, I pull him down on top of me. He groans as our bodies connect, and I begin moving.

"Fate, if you don't stop I'm going to go to my happy place without even having to get naked," he says, and I can't help but giggle. "You think that's funny?" he says as he gives me this devilish grin. Slowly, his hands creep up, and I know what he's going to do before he even touches me. I break out in a fit of laughter before he even has his hands on me to tickle me. Usually, I'd panic at such a touch, but all I'm doing is trying to breathe through the laughter.

"Please stop," I say in laughter, and he jumps off me. He thinks he's done something wrong, so before he can figure out what I'm really thinking, I jump over to him and begin tickling him. He falls back against the couch, and I climb on top of him, continuing my assault as he chuckles against me, trying to grab my hands. "Do you give in?" I say while I'm giggling and continuing to tickle him.

He gives me a warning glare, and I stop. "If I say yes, does that mean you are going to get off of me?" I giggle again, then he pulls me down to him and kisses me again.

"We have to stop or I won't get to see you school me in the world of fish," he says when he pulls away.

"Fine, if that's what you want. Prepare to be educated, Mr. McAlister," I say with a grin on my face.

I'VE BEEN TO AQUARIUMS before. I lived in Orlando, so water and fish are kind of everywhere, but being here with Cameron is something different. Other than with Clarissa, I've never really shared my love of marine life. No one ever really wanted to know me. The walls I'd built up over the years kept people away. That is one of the reasons I had those walls, to keep people out, but also to keep out the memories and protect me from new harms. As soon as we are through the door, the comfort that nature brings me engulfs my senses.

Even though this isn't natural, it is still beautiful. These are creatures we wouldn't have easy access to in their true homes without diving, so this gives everyone a chance to enjoy the wonders of the waters.

Making our way into the first room of exhibits, we see the hippos, jellyfish, and octopus. Cameron seems to be fascinated with the colorful display the jellyfish exhibit has. He never lets go of my hand the whole way through as we weave between the crowds. When we get to the shark exhibit I pull away and walk up to the glass, placing both hands against the glass. They are predators, but they still live in a community. It's amazing to see the workings of that up close. Turning, I notice Cameron is watching me with a smile on his face.

"Seeing you here, it's as if I'm on the inside of those walls with you, getting to see you clearly," he says, and my heart melts. The ice princess he'd called me out on being the day we met has become less and less since he walked into my world. Leaving the glass, I walk up to him and wrap my arms around him.

"Oh, my God," a girl screeches from next to us, and her eyes are locked on Cameron and me. "You are Cameron McAlister from Ten Ways Gone," she says, getting louder as she goes on. Cameron gets protective and tries to get me out of sight, but I don't budge. "And you're Fate," she yells, and I slightly flinch, but I don't think Cameron notices. "You guys are so freaking cute together!" Maybe this girl should find some place to sit down before she passes out from excitement.

Cameron is tense, and I know he doesn't know what to do or say because I'm with him. *Screw it world, I'm here.* "Thank you," I say with a smile. "Would you like me to take a picture for you with him?"

"Oh!" The girl gasps and sways on her feet as her eyes bug out. Then she's jumping up and down "Really?" She is jumping up and down. I laugh softly, and I sense a bit of the tension draining from Cameron. "Wait." She waves to a woman who must be with her and hands this person her phone. "Can I get a picture with both of you?"

What? Come on, Fate, can't back out now. "Of course," I say and smile, then I glance at Cameron, who is just watching me with an odd expression. We pose for the picture, and the girl thanks us before heading off on her way again.

Cameron is still staring at me, slack-jawed with shock reflecting in his eyes.

"What's wrong?" I ask.

"Nothing is wrong. I just can't believe it." He shakes his head with a little chuckle. "I was panicking thinking you were going to shut down because someone recognized us, but you just soared. I know you don't want to go public yet, but when you do, they are going to care for you just as much as I do." His carefully chosen words warm my soul because every day we find new triggers, and he just rolls with those punches. He is careful of his words and actions so that I'm at ease.

I'm in deeper than I could have imagined.

"So where is the French Angel Fish?" Cameron asks, and it takes me a moment to know why he's asking about that particular fish. "I want to see what we have. I bet it will be amazing to watch. I'm sure the world is jealous of us," he says, joking.

"Well, I'm not sure if they have any here. They

don't have every fish or marine animal. Each aquarium has different things to attract different audiences. Plus, there are just too many in the ocean to cram them into one aquarium," I say as we continue walking through the exhibits. Cameron sees something and begins pulling me in another direction. I have no option but to follow him away from the walls of the sea turtle exhibit I was currently staring at. When he pulls me in front of the exhibit, and my chest tighten.

"We might not have the monogamous French Angel Fish, but we do have these. The book you gave me talked about them as well. They share the load of life's hardships so they both can survive. I know these aren't the exact ones from the book, but my meaning is the same."

Glancing through the glass, every bit of his words hits home for me. *Penguins.* Tears sting at my eyes then break free. There are people around going about the attractions, but it's like we are alone here.

"Some things are far too precious to let go, and they know that too," he says, and a few tears slip out. He wipes them away and just stares at me.

"Actually, most penguins are monogamous. These African penguins can be too, but the emperor penguin is the most monogamous penguin," I blurt out, and he chuckles.

"I know, I read about them. Something like fifteen percent stay together in the next mating season, but that's due to circumstances of being torn apart by death or the elements." I smile at him in amazement. Never has someone taken such an interest in something so close to me. "We are that fifteen percent, Fate, because I'm not going to let anything pull us apart."

"I'm sorry to interrupt such a beautiful moment." Turning, a lady in her late fifties is watching us with tears in her eyes. She has a uniform on, indicating that she works here, and the penguin pin tells me that this is her exhibit. "We do have French Angel Fish. They are in the exhibit right down that hall on your left." Cameron snickers, and I can't help but smile at us being caught in our crazy fish moment. Cameron grabs my hand again and turns me to him. He lightly presses his lips to mine. "Most certainly a monogamous creature you have there, miss. You enjoy your day here at the aquarium." Cameron continues to lead me through the exhibits and my world finally feels complete with him here with me in my other happy place.

On our way back to the apartment we get out of the cab early and walk, enjoying each other's company. Being here with Cameron, having him understand my insecurities, is like my world finally makes sense again. No more nightmares, no more fear, because each day we find a new way to work them out. Things I don't want him to see or know come out, and he just shows me how much I mean to him every time. Nothing could take me off the cloud his actions and words put me on.

"Hello, Fate."

Just like that I'm in my nightmares with him, but I know I'm not sleeping. I'm staring at him in the light of the day. He really is out, and he has found me.

Chapter Twenty-Seven

Fate

"Fate, who is this man?" Cameron asks.

I'm frozen in place, unable to move, unable to even breathe.

"Fate."

I stare at him, and I can't even say our word to tell him how much of a struggle this is. Protectively, he takes a step so he is a bit in front of me, telling me that he knows without me saying it. "Who are you?"

"Tsk, tsk. Is that any way to talk to your girlfriend's father?"

Cameron's eyes go big and I want to pull away. Run away like my body is telling me to, but Cameron's touch has me pinned.

"What, aren't you going to give Daddy a hug? I missed my baby girl," he says in a snide tone, and I'm instantly nauseated as my stomach rolls.

My eyes dart to the left, glancing at Cameron. *I'm going to have to do this, I can't have him see me this way. Not him.* I take a step forward, but Cameron tugs me back to him.

My father notices, and his eyes narrow to slits as anger changes his face. "I want a moment alone with my daughter, if you please."

I'm silently praying that Cameron will just let this go. Knowing will destroy us.

"Kurt, I think you've had enough alone moments with your daughter already, don't you?" My stomach drops at Cameron's words. Frantically, my eyes find his, and I know then the secret I thought I was keeping he already knew.

"Who are you to tell me what I can do with my daughter?" my father says, enraged.

"I don't have to tell you shit, the law told you that. I think you need to just walk away, Kurt, or this will end badly. Trust me when I say you will never touch her again."

Darkness edges into my vision as the world closes in around me. This is it, the end of my life. Cameron is standing here telling me that he knows all my secrets. "How?" I whisper, my eyes finding the ground.

His hand lightly touches my chin, bringing my eyes to be level with his and my heart stills. His blue eyes are penetrating right through me like there isn't anything between us. Like he's not here, but I know he's watching this. "The first night you had a nightmare you were screaming, but you also kept saying 'Daddy, no.' I wasn't sure what you were talking about. However, the more I got to know you, I just had this sick feeling in my stomach that he had done something to you." I try to pull my face out of his grip in shame, but he doesn't let me. "I wasn't sure until I saw your face just now." He bends down to me so only I can hear him. "He will never touch you again, Fate, no one will. I promise you that."

"How cute," my father says, reminding us he's

178

here. "I've done my time because of that. Nothing says I can't have a relationship with my daughter now." The word relationship slides off his tongue, so filled with innuendo, I want to hurl. My world is spinning. I'm trapped. "Especially since the world now knows what a whore she is. Screwing a rock star is a step up, sweetheart, just don't forget your roots."

Cameron stiffens. I'm not sure what he's thinking. He's closed down, shut me out, and that is the worst feeling in the world. Tugging my hand as hard as I can, I wrench from his grasp and instantly fear takes hold of me. He goes to glare at me, but my eyes dart to the ground since I can't bear to have him see me right now. The look of disgust would destroy me.

"Stay away from Fate," Cameron roars.

"Good for you, son, protecting that nice piece of ass you found yourself." I now notice Kurt's words are a bit slurred and, now that he is close enough to me, I can smell the booze coming from him. He's had a relapse. This isn't the father I grew up with for nine years, it's the monster that the booze made him into after my mother died. Cameron moves so fast I miss it and he is on top of him, his fists colliding with my father's face.

"Cameron, no!" I scream. People are staring and taking pictures, and more come around to see what the hollering is about. Quickly, I rush to him. "Cameron, please stop." My words aren't getting through to him, and I know I have no choice. Just as I go to grab him, his elbow connects with my left shoulder and I'm thrown back. My head snaps back as I hit the ground, smashing into the sidewalk, and for a moment I'm lightheaded.

Trying to pick myself up, Cameron just stares at

me. I know that all his fears about his anger have just happened. I know he wants to come to me, but he's holding back. He's doing what I do. His thoughts are full of blame.

My father begins to get to his feet, and he is watching the scene in front of him. "Guess I'm not the only abuser," Kurt insults.

Cameron gets ready to go to the deep end of his anger again. Just before he lunges, I yell, "Choose." Just like that, all the anger disperses, and he turns, frowning at me with such sorrow that it pulls on my soul.

"Choose what?" Kurt says, clearly confused.

Leaning into my father so others can't hear, he says, "None of your business. You have no business here. Do you get it? I will fucking kill you before I ever let you touch her again." The anger is building, and I know I need to get him out of here. Grabbing Cameron, I try to show him with my eyes that I need to leave. Pulling, he eventually gives in and lets me lead him away.

"Maybe I'll kill her first. Those pictures aren't doing it for me anymore, and I won't go back to jail for a little bitch," he slurs.

Cameron stops in his tracks, but I put my hand on his chest. He brushes me off and the loss of him right away turns my body to ice.

"He's not worth it," I plead.

"You're right, none of this shit is," he snaps back, and I flinch. He takes off, walking away from me.

"Dad, get some help and stay the hell away from me. Stop ruining my life," I scream and run off after Cameron. When I round the corner on the way to our building, I can't see him anywhere. Cameron is nowhere to be seen. I take off as fast as I can, picking up the pace as I head to our apartment. After I unlock the door and step inside, I find that I'm by myself. His door is open and I know he hasn't been back here yet. I throw my bag on the table and fall against the wall. My body is making itself a puddle on the floor and I pray for tears, but they never come. I'm broken. My phone begins to ring, and I scramble to answer it. "Cameron?" I say hopefully.

"Fate, it's Clarissa." I gasp at the realization it isn't Cameron calling me. *Cameron, no.* "Fate, what's wrong?" I don't speak. There is so much to say, but I have no words. "Fate, if you don't answer me right now, I'm getting on a plane. Fate," Clarissa yells.

"Cameron's gone," I whimper.

"Fate, start from the beginning," she pleads.

"Kurt was here. Cameron attacked him after he figured out what had happened between us. I got him off of him, but he accidentally knocked me over, and then when I finally got him to leave, Kurt said…" I can't finish, my throat feels like it's closing up. Clarissa doesn't even know the extent of it.

"What? Tell me, Fate," she begs.

"He said he'd kill me before he'd go back to jail again and…" Taking a deep breath, I give her my final secret, "that the pictures aren't keeping him as good of company as I would."

"What kind of pictures, Fate?" she cries out, and my heart breaks for her in this moment.

I've had years of these memories, and I know I can barely handle them. "He has pictures of me without my clothes on in my room," I say.

"He says he still has them? Why didn't you tell

me about this when it happened?" she asks, trying to remain calm, but I can hear the soft sobs coming from the other side of the phone.

"He says he does. Clarissa, he's drinking again. I could smell it on him, and he was slurring his words."

She understands what this means when it comes to that man. "I'm getting on a plane right now." I can hear her shuffling around and then the sound of the clicking of a keyboard. "There isn't a flight until tomorrow morning," she says in frustration.

"You don't have to come, Clarissa."

"I know I don't have to, but I am coming. There's no use arguing about it," she says firmly, and if I wasn't dying inside right now, I might feel some relief at her coming. "It's going to be okay, Fate."

"Cameron," I whisper.

"It's a lot to take in, Fate. He'll be back," she says, trying to lessen my pain.

"It's over, he's not coming back. He knows the truth and he can't handle it. No one can. This is why I pushed him away before. Why I broke down and had to be committed, because I knew this moment would come and I would be feeling this. He finally knows and can't look at me," I say and I believe every word.

"Then he isn't who I thought he was, and he isn't the person for you, but I think you're wrong," Clarissa says.

A bang echoes through the room, and I gasp.

"Fate," Clarissa yells from the phone, but I can't say a word.

"Cameron," I cry out, and tears glide down my face. He is just standing there, watching me. The pain I'm seeing in his face mirrors the pain inside of me.

"Fate, are you crying?" Clarissa gasps.

"Yes, I'm crying. He's here, Clarissa," I whisper, scared that if I'm too loud I might startle him or wake up and find out he's not really here. "I have to go."

"Listen to me, let him tell you what he feels, don't assume, and you have to let him talk about this. You can't ignore this. The cat's out of the bag so to speak. He might have questions. But you have to trust him to stay. I love you, and I'll see you tomorrow at eleven o'clock."

I don't even have to hang up as the click tells me she has. I just let the phone fall from my hands to the ground beside me.

"Fate." He sighs and starts to take small steps toward me. When he gets close enough to me, he bends down so he's down on the floor with me. Slowly, he brings his hand up like he's going to touch me, but he changes his mind and withdraws his hand. The agony slices through me.

Without thinking, I let everything Clarissa told me slip from my mind. "I wouldn't want to touch me either," I say with disgust.

"Fate," he chokes out, and I feel it then. The loss.

Chapter Twenty-Eight

Cameron

When I walked in and saw her, I was wrecked. My girl was huddled up like her world was destroyed. I destroyed her. My anger got the better of me, and I hurt her. Then I took off because I was so blinded by my rage I didn't want her to get caught in the crossfire again. That was worse. I only got so far before I realized who I had left her there with. I'm an asshole. The moment I went back and saw she wasn't there, and neither was he, I lost my damn mind.

I wanted to reach out and pull her to me the moment I saw her, but I don't deserve that. Protecting her was the one thing I was supposed to do, and I failed her. My rage clouded that need, and I will never forgive myself for that. Now she's sitting here in pieces because she thinks I'm revolted by her.

"Fate," I choke out, and the emotions within me are trying to break free. "I am so sorry," I whisper to her, and she nods her head. My girl sits here shattered, like a child needing protection. That monster did this. This is what he made her feel like all those night, and by running, I wasn't there to shelter her. To keep her in the now and out of that hell he brought her. My stomach turns and I think I'm going to throw up. Sick bastard.

"I don't blame you. You didn't ask for this, any of this, and some things are just too much to overlook. I'm just too tainted," she states, and I crash.

Those tears I am barely holding in begin to fall. "You are so stupid," I say when I finally get my breath steady. She reaches out wiping away the tears in my eyes that are identical to hers. "I didn't leave to get away from you, I was trying to get a check on my anger because I wanted to kill him and I hurt you. I don't deserve these tears. I know you don't cry for shit, so to see you like this is damn near killing me. Please, babe, stop crying. Talk to me, don't shut me out." I'm begging her to just let those walls down and bring me in. "I don't care if you shut the world out, but shut me in there with you," I say, hoping it gets through to her.

"It's a pretty scary place to be. Are you sure you really want to know?" she whimpers, and I want to end this here. I wish I could take this pain away from her.

"Nothing you're going to tell me will change anything. I can promise you that, Fate. You could never say anything to make me not love you." She gasps at my proclamation of my feelings. Not because I don't feel it, but because I know she can't say it back and that will eat at her. She needs to hear it now. Someone needs to show this beautifully destroyed girl that they love her no matter what, and I'll be damned if I'm going to let someone who isn't me be that person for her.

"After my mother died, my father began drinking. I remember him drinking when I was a bit younger, but he went away for a while and when he came back everything was fine. I assume he went to rehab. After my mom died, he relapsed and started drinking every day. My mother's death destroyed him," she says. As she speaks, I can see right inside to that scared little girl. "He came into my room one night and…" I can sense her panic coming on and I want to comfort her, but I don't know how without more pain for her. "He molested me until I finally told someone and they took me away. He went to jail, and I never saw him again until today."

Pieces begin to come together in my head of the things she's said.

"He only came at night in the dark," I say, and she nods. "Music, how does that come into this?" I ask because we have been working on it and now pushed where I never should have.

"I would scream or call out for help. So he started turning on music before he came in and woke me. It's why I panicked when I woke to your music being on."

So much makes sense now. Hell, I wish I had known. I could have done things so differently.

"It's why I don't cry. He either liked that he had that power over me or it would only make things worse. So I stopped crying. I got out before he could have…"

That annihilates my heart. I've made this gorgeous girl cry a few times that I know about, so for that to have happened, I must have brought her so much pain. That asshole took from her everything, and she has never known a loving touch since that day. Luckily, she got out before he could…*Damn it.* That eats at me. "I don't care what that animal did to you. You were a child, Fate. Do you hear me? You didn't ask for this shit, and he has no excuse. Don't give him one. He was your dad. His job was to protect you. The only blame and disgust is for him. Never you."

With my words, she grabs my hand, giving it a tight squeeze. Those walls come crashing down, and it's as if I can finally breathe again.

"You aren't just saying that, are you? I don't need pretend shit, Cameron."

Damn, I love it when she swears at me. It makes me feel like I'm rubbing off on her, and that makes her mine. "Look at me, Fate." Her eyes lock with mine, they are swollen and red. She's never been more beautiful to me because I can see the real Fate, without all the bullshit she puts up to protect herself. "I don't do pretend shit, not with you. I love you, so get that through that adorably thick head of yours and stop pushing me out. I. Am. Not. Going. Anywhere," I say firmly. "Do you hear me? No matter what comes, I'm not leaving. You're going to have to make me and even then, no. There will never be another Fate for me, but you. I fucking love you."

"I…" I can see her struggling, and I know what she's trying to do.

Panic takes me over as I think she might break down again, and I hate that my love could do that to her. Not again. She feels like she has to say it back. "Fate, don't. I didn't say it for you to say it back. Someone can say it, and they don't need the words to know it's real, okay? I will never love anyone as much as I love you, and I don't need to hear you say it right now."

"Say it again," she whispers.

"I. Fucking. Love. You."

Slowly, she begins to move toward me until she is so close we are almost touching. Her breathing increases, and she is making me so damn nervous. Then she says something I never thought I'd hear. "Touch me, please. Make it all go away."

Shaking my head, I try to back away, but she only moves forward, closing the distance between us. "I can't. You're upset and this might make it worse. I couldn't handle losing you, Fate," I say, begging her.

"The need is all I feel, the need to wash it all away. To start new, and please, just…" She has never been so sexy, and she is here before me, broken, asking me to make her whole. She pauses briefly, and my mind is spinning. "Love me, Cameron. Touch me. Please make me yours."

Slowly, so I don't spook her, I bring my hands behind her head and her lips to mine. When they meet her lips are soft and swollen, and I have to hold back. She begins moving her lips against mine, increasing the intensity. This girl is going to be the death of me. Her hands move and she lays them against my chest. The heat from her touch burns right through my shirt, and then she begins to trail her fingers down to the hem of my shirt and grazes them against my bare skin. I groan as she caresses me, and she takes that chance to deepen the kiss, her tongue moving against mine.

Fate tugs the hem of my shirt upward, and I pull back briefly to allow her to lift it over my head. She reaches for the bottom of her shirt, and I watch as she brings it up and quickly discards it. I don't even have a chance to enjoy the view before she is climbing on top of me, almost straddling me. She starts kissing me again with only her pants and bra still on. She pushes her hands against my chest, pushing me back down to the floor and she follows me down, never breaking our kiss. *God damn it.*

"Cameron," she moans, and without thinking, I place my hands on the bare skin of her back. I wait for her to flinch, but it never happens. Instead, she moves against me, her whole body grinding against mine. Hell, I almost lose it right there.

"Fate, we have to stop," I plead with her. Shit, I only have so much control.

"Why?" she murmurs.

"Fate, I only have so much willpower. At some point, I won't be able to stop. I already don't want to," I say honestly, hoping she understands how much control she has over me.

"Then don't," she says and tries to kiss me again, but I pull back. Holding her face in my hands, I try to connect with her eyes to see what my girl is thinking. I've never seen this side of her.

"Do you have any idea how much you control me? You could bring me to my knees at any moment. That's how much. I don't think I could stop loving you if we don't slow down." Never have I sounded like such a pussy, but I don't even care. This girl needs to know how real this is for me.

"Love me, Cameron," she says, with her eyes keeping me in place as she climbs back on top of me, placing her hands around my shoulders. "If I'm in control, then do what I say. It's time you fucking love me, Cameron McAlister."

Yeah, that's it. All willpower is blown out of the water. I grab her legs, wrapping them around my waist. Grasping onto her hips, I bring us up from the floor and move us to my bed. Slowly, I lay her down before positioning myself over her. She unfastens my pants, and I groan at her touch. Her hands wrap around my waist as she slips her hands in my pants. *Did she just grab my ass? Shit.* She begins to slide my pants down and I kick them off, never breaking away from kissing her. This girl needs to feel how much I love her. I need her to never doubt that for a fucking minute of this.

Gently, I bring my hands down to her waist and slowly move my fingers to the button on her jeans. I'm almost losing it here because my girl has her hands firmly on my ass like she's claiming me as hers. *Damn right, baby, I'm all yours.* I groan, and she quivers against me.

"Oh, Cameron," she says as I slip her pants and panties off, touching her the whole way down. Gazing at me with this cute little smirk on her face, she says, "We're naked. Now what, rock star?"

"There's no going back from here, Fate," I say, because I can't believe this girl is naked before me, asking me to be with her. Trailing my hand down her stomach, I continue down until I'm right where she wants me to be. I slip inside, and she moans, digging her hands into my back, and that only further entices me. Slowly, I move until she is comfortable with my fingers being inside her. Each time I pick up the pace, her breathing gets more intense. One of her hands runs up and down my back. The other hand strokes me, and nothing can compare to being touched by Fate.

"I don't ever want to go back to a place without you, without this with you," she whispers, and I stop what I'm doing. Grasping both her hands with one of mine, I put them just above her head as I balance myself above her.

"I won't let you," I promise her and release her

hands. I don't want her feeling trapped in this moment. I just want her to feel us. "This might hurt at first. I'll be gentle." As I lower myself to her, I never break eye contact. "It's just me and you, babe," I whisper as I slip inside her and groan. She is so damn tight, I'm scared to move and hurt her. Gently, I push through her barrier and get a rhythm going. "Always," I groan as I find myself going deeper inside of her. It's like finally coming home, and I never want to leave.

"Cameron," she says, and she arches against me to bring us closer. There isn't an inch between us. My hand moves to her breast and she closes her eyes, moaning loudly as she places her head against my chest. "*Forever in a day* is what I feel." Her words rip through me. Those are lyrics I wrote about her and it tells me all I need to hear. This girl loves me.

She tightens around me, and it has me slowing down as I gently push myself in and out. "Don't stop," she says, and I want to groan out in frustration. I want her to enjoy this, and I'm ready to bury myself in her. "I...I'm almost there," she moans as her nails dig into me. She tightens around me again and I love it. I bury myself in her, not stopping, loving every beat as she comes undone beneath me.

"I love you, Fate," I moan as I find my release with the girl who has ruined me for the rest of the world. There will never be another Fate. Her fingers trail across my face, and I lean into her touch.

"Forever in a day," she whispers as she moves over, and I cuddle up beside my world.

Just as she's drifting off into sleep, I whisper to her, "One day I'm going to make you mine in more ways than this. Forever in a day, babe." Placing my hands on her, I settle into a peaceful sleep with my *Fate*.

WE HAVEN'T BEEN ASLEEP long when knocking at the door wakes us. I slowly pull on a pair of jogging pants and hand Fate one of my shirts to put on.

"Who is it?" she asks.

I just shrug in response. *Who the hell knocks on a door at this time?* When I open the door, I'm floored as to what is in front of us.

Two police officers are standing there and, before I even have a chance to say anything, one of them speaks. "Cameron McAlister?"

I nod.

"You have to come with us. You are under arrest for the assault of Kurt Bishop."

Fate cries out, and the officers put me up against the door and cuff me. The whole time I can hear Fate wailing behind me, and there is nothing I can do for her now.

Chapter Twenty-Nine

Fate

BEING IN THE POLICE station is freaking me out. I can't stay still, so I'm pacing back and forth. Nothing prepared me for that knock on the door. I thought it was Clarissa, that she had taken an earlier flight. As soon as I got here I called Scott and Cecilia and they both showed up raising hell. I couldn't get a hold of Clarissa to tell her because she was already through security and on board before I thought to call her, but I left her a voicemail saying I was here.

An officer comes and asks me to come into an interview room. I follow without question. I go in and the officer shuts the door, leaving me alone with another officer who was waiting for me inside of the room. Taking my seat, I try to remain calm, but being in here brings me back to when I had to do all this because my father was being arrested and charged.

"Miss McKenzie, my name is Officer Davidson. I was wondering if I could speak with you about what happened last night between your boyfriend and your father," he asks, and I find myself telling him how the incident happened while he is jotting it down. "So you felt threatened?" he asks.

"Yes, my father was drunk and was making comments about killing me before going back to jail. He is still on parole, I believe, and he wasn't supposed to be here anyway. Cameron's actions were a result of his fear for my safety and my father provoking him with his vulgarities of the sexual abuse I endured as a child. Then, after the fight broke apart, my father again tried to provoke Cameron by disclosing that he still had pictures of me as a child, inappropriate pictures." The words just flow from my mouth as if it's nothing. I'm numb.

"Your father admitted to having child pornography?" I nod my head, and he continues to write on his pad. "Well, he's going back to jail. He broke parole by coming here, and the local police will be doing a search of all of his possessions. If he has those pictures, we will find them and that will be another charge," he says, and I'm relieved that my father is again returning to the cell he deserves.

"What about Cameron?" I ask.

"With your witness of the events in question, we will be dropping the charges as I believe he acted in your defense. I'm sure your father won't be pushing too hard for those charges to stick either. We should be able to get Mr. McAlister released in a couple of hours." The officer brings me back out to the lobby and leaves me with Cecilia and Scott.

Without thinking, I walk over to Cecilia and hug her. She stiffens at the contact from me. Softly, her arms wrap around me, giving me a warm embrace. It doesn't calm me instantly like Cameron, but it makes me feel as if I'm not alone. I fall apart and the sobs return.

"Fate." The voice comes from behind me.

I turn and spot Clarissa. She looks as rough as I am feeling right now. Leaving Cecilia, I walk up to her, crying, and see the same emotion has tears pooling in her eyes too.

"Oh, Fate, honey, it will be okay."

I hope she's right. That this is just one more stop on the train of chaos for us, but I have this nagging feeling in my chest that it's not that simple. Clarissa pulls me into a hug, and I let her. "Thank you for coming."

"Fate, you don't have to thank me. I will always come running when you need me." Pulling back, she searches my eyes. Then, with a shaky smile, she slips a tissue from her purse and dabs at my tears. "It is okay to need someone, honey." She knows how hard that is for me, and I surprise her when I finally speak.

"I need Cameron."

"I'm here, babe," Cameron whispers behind me and I turn around. As soon as we lock eyes I take off running until I'm crashing into his arms. I finally let go, but the tears seem endless. "Everything is all worked out, and you're here in my damn arms again where you belong," he says, as he gives me a tight squeeze. "We are going to be okay."

"We should get out of here," Scott says, and Cameron nods. Cameron never lets go of me as we walk out of the police station. It's as if he can feel it too, so much has changed. Cecilia suggests we go to her place, but Cameron says no and that he wants to get me back home. Clarissa stays closely beside me until we reach her rental car.

"Are you coming, Fate?" she asks as Cameron glances at the cab he just waved down. Something in his eyes tells me he wants to be alone with me and I need that too.

"I'm going to go with Cameron. You get settled in the hotel, then come to our place." She hesitates before getting into her rental. I know she wants to argue, but I'm happy she lets it go. I can't really handle anything else right now. Getting into the cab with Cameron, it's like everything around us is about to change.

Walking into our apartment, it's as if these last few days haven't happened. Just another nightmare I woke up from, but I know it's not because I could not have dreamed what happened last night with Cameron. "Fate, I'm sorry I ruined our night."

"What are you talking about? I should be the one apologizing. You got arrested because of me."

"I wanted it to be perfect, and I wish it didn't happen this way because it's just turned to shit."

"Don't say that," I cry out to him, and he winces in pain. "When I walked in here all I was thinking about was that these last few days have been like my nightmares, but you know how I know I wasn't in one of them?" He just stares at me not saying anything. "Because of what happened between us. So please, don't try to take it back because it's the only good I have to hold on to right now." I pray he doesn't continue with his regretful thoughts, because each one is like a new pain in my chest.

"Fate, I want to take it back for you. So the first time isn't surrounded by this sadness. Not the actual event because, damn, babe, I could never forget being with you. You've ruined me for the world. I was all about Fate before that happened, and now I know every inch of you. Every inch of you that now belongs to only me."

His words make me squirm under his gaze and

every part of my body ignites. "I do," I whisper, and he cocks his head to the side in response. "I belong to you, every piece of me belongs to you, Cameron."

"Fuck," he says in a heavy breath as he brings his hand around my back, pulling me to him. His lips push against mine and I open up, letting him in. His hands find their way under the hem of my shirt, sending a trail of warmth following his hands as they slide across my skin. Quickly, he pulls away, and I groan in frustration. "Fate, I want to, trust me. I need this as badly as you do, but they will be here soon, and I have to figure out all this shit before they get here with questions."

Just like that, everything comes rushing back. All the pain and problems I've brought on Cameron by having him in my life. The dread that overtakes my body has my hands shaking as I say the words that crush me. "Maybe we shouldn't do that again."

Cameron gasps as I pull away from him, walking into the living room. "What the hell do you mean by that, Fate?" Cameron is pulling his hand through his hair, and all the pain in his eyes only tells me how bad this really is.

"Us, all this crap that surrounds it. All it's doing is messing up your life. You were arrested only a few hours ago. What if they hadn't dropped the charges, Cameron?" My heart hurts just at the thought of that. "I couldn't live with myself if something happened to you and it was all my fault. My life put yours in jeopardy, and I can't have that."

"Fate," he pleads.

"You don't need this in your life, Cameron." My words remain firm, and I do not go to him.

"This shit means nothing to me. I don't care about

it. I'd do it all over again because that is what you do when you love someone."

Trying to get a handle on my tears, I want badly to try to finally let the world in. Standing there in Cameron's arms, I'm safe again, like nothing can penetrate us here in our safe bubble. It's over. The charges are dropped and my father is back where he belongs.

There is a knock at the door, then Scott, Cecilia, and Clarissa come walking in. "Cameron, we have a problem," Scott says, and his face is full of dread. Glancing at me, he can barely keep eye contact. I watch as he hands Cameron his phone and nothing could prepare me for what is on the screen.

There are pictures of the fighting with my father, Cameron being released, and finally him and me walking out of the police station together. Scrolling through the words everything stops. They have my father's name. My body freezes as the words sexual offender stand out, but it's as if I'm going to faint when read that last line. *What else has Fate been hiding?*

Chapter Thirty

Fate

"Fate, you should come home with me. This is too much, honey," Clarissa says, and my body runs cold.

"What? No," Cameron says firmly. "This is her home. You can't just take her. She has school, and we are—" He appears so lost.

"Cameron, I appreciate your input, but really, this doesn't concern you. This is about Fate. This isn't something she can handle. You must know that. Having her name out there was the reason he was even able to find her. Now they might ask questions about her history. Do you really want that for her?" Clarissa says, and her attitude reminds me of our days together when she was just my worker.

"Of course not," he says firmly. "I would do anything to keep her from this."

"Then let her go," Clarissa begs, and my heart is crashing.

"Never, I can't. I won't," he declares, and I'm overwhelmed by all the emotions this arguing is bringing out in me. "I love her. I can't just let her go, Clarissa. I'm sorry my name got her into this, but I'm not sorry I love her. I won't be without her. I love her too much." His words feel so distant to me right now; the stress from this tension is overtaking my body. "I'll handle this. You don't have to worry. I'll make this go away."

"That sounds like a selfish rock star who is only thinking about himself and not the person he loves. What are you going to do, Cameron, throw some money at them? If you could make this go away you would have as soon as they found out who she was," Clarissa tells Cameron, and the distance between these people and myself growing with each word.

"Are you serious?" Cecilia says, and I know this is going to only get worse. "He has done everything he can to protect her. He didn't go public with their relationship for her because she wasn't ready to be labeled the rock star's new love interest. You don't know anything about what's going on here. So I think you need to back off."

"She shouldn't have to be labeled anything. She's just a young woman starting out, and this world is going to swallow her up and spit her out. You don't know what it's like for her. I do, and I'm saying she needs to come home."

Cecilia is fuming at Clarissa's comments. "I think you don't know anything about what it's like for her *now*. You knew the Fate you dropped off here at the beginning of the year, but she isn't that girl anymore. Don't pretend that what we have with her means nothing, because you are wrong, Clarissa."

I can't keep listening to this. Walking into his bedroom, leaving everyone behind, I can hear them still arguing about it. Scott is the only one who isn't saying anything, but I doubt it's because he doesn't have anything to say. In confrontations, I've noticed he only speaks when it's necessary, that way it's valued as important. Cecilia is on Cameron's side, but Clarissa just isn't backing down.

"We all should stop before any of you say anything else you regret," Scott says, and I'm glad he's trying to divert the situation. "None of what any of us thinks matters anyway. It's Fate's life, it's her choice." No one responds, but the sound of footsteps tells me I've been followed into Cameron's bedroom.

"Fate," Cameron speaks, and it only brings the memories of last night back. Feeling him against me, the love he showed me and the love I know is still ahead of us, makes me feel safe.

"Can we have a moment alone, please?" I say to everyone. Clarissa is hesitant but leaves with Scott and Cecilia. Cameron, however, has this vulnerable expression on his face that I know all too well. I'm sure it's on my face all the time. Sitting on the bed, I relive all of it again. My memories of the night before continue to play out in my head until Cameron pulls me from them.

"I love you," he says. "Forever in a day, remember?"

"School is ending. We haven't talked about it, but maybe now we should."

Cameron comes and sits beside me, placing his hand over mine. "What does school ending have to do with us?"

Has he never thought of what would happen at the end of this semester? "We can't stay here. We have to move out for the summer. Where does that leave us? Me in Orlando and you wherever your music takes you. Maybe we took this too far," I say honestly.

"Don't say that. What we have is perfect. It's forever, Fate. I never thought about the semester ending because it doesn't change a thing for me. If you want to go home for the summer and have your life back there, I get that. We can just apply to be roommates again for next year. I will visit you and love you every moment, but I'm really hoping you go with my other option for you," he says, and my heart stills. "Let's get a house. Our home. One we don't have to say goodbye to at the end of every school year. One we get to come back to and call home after the tour. Stay with me, visit Orlando, but make your home with me." Could it be that easy for us? Nothing else has been, so why this? "Let me love you, and I swear no one will ever love you like I do. Please, babe. This is our fate."

He stands there in silence, waiting for me to say something to him, but I remain silent. Words would not be enough to explain everything I'm feeling. Pulling him to me, I kiss him, his soft lips hesitating against mine, but that quickly dissolves, and he deepens the kiss. When I break away, there is pain in his eyes and I want to take it all away.

"Tell me that wasn't a goodbye."

Before me is the boy who sometimes shines through from his rock star appearance. "Fate doesn't say goodbye." He gazes at me confused, and I realize he might think I'm talking about myself. "Some things are destined to happen whether people want them to or not. Once those things do happen, it is fate. Cameron, we are fated. I can't promise it will be easy, because the best things aren't. So let's push through it all. What I'm saying is, my home is where you are.

Chapter Thirty-One

Fate

BEING IN THE APARTMENT without Cameron seemed weird. I didn't tell him, but once he was gone I just couldn't sleep at night again. The media coverage of the incident with my father hasn't blown over. If anything, they just have more questions. It's not like it's hard to find out information about registered sexual offenders. At least the victims aren't stuck in that category, but it's been thrown out there that maybe I was abused in some manner.

When that happened, Cameron came home to me screaming and throwing things in my room. I think I scared him more than anything, but since then he's been distant. A few days later, something came up and he had to go to California for work. He had asked if I wanted to visit Clarissa, but honestly, I was hurt he didn't ask me to go with him. Classes where finished other than reviewing, and it wasn't a problem to miss at this point.

He came back just in time for exams and he was different. Distant. That wasn't like anything I'd ever experienced with Cameron, and it worried me. Cecilia kept telling me I was over thinking things and men are men, but something didn't sit right with me. Even when he was stressed or concerned about things, he never shut me out. It just wasn't like Cameron to do that to me. I'd asked him if something was wrong, and he continuously told me nothing was going on. I didn't have much choice but to trust him. He'd never led me astray before.

Sitting in the middle of the floor, I continue with what I've been working on since the day he left. Cameron was gone and I had no one to take baby steps with, so I started finding ways to do them myself. Music was my baby step. The first few times were difficult. I'd seen the band practice, but I wasn't alone. I could see Cameron and I had Cecilia with me. She would distract me if she saw me getting overwhelmed, and Cameron was only a few steps away at all times.

I started out listening to his album in the living room with all the lights on, and I can't tell you how many times I had to turn it off and relax before trying again. I eventually found that if I focused on Cameron's voice it was easy to picture him there with me and that helped immensely. Once he came back, I moved it to my bedroom and I did it when he was gone. I wasn't hiding it from him, but this was something I was doing by myself. Tonight he had to meet the band, as they had to get some last minute things together for the tour.

When it got dark, I moved into my room to read. I also started working on removing lights from the situation. One at a time, I got the lights down to just one. My desk lamp is all that is on in the entire apartment, and it is pitch black outside. I can hear the other residents all out there having their end of the year parties, so I turn up my music to drown them out.

An hour later my door busts open and I yelp in surprise. In front of me is Cameron, who is breathing heavy. His eyes are full of fear, and that brings me into a panic. "Cameron, what's wrong?" I say, putting my book down and climbing out of my bed toward him, turning the music down as I pass it.

"I..." He pauses and glances around. "What the hell are you doing, Fate?" he asks questioningly.

"I'm reading?"

"In an almost all dark apartment with music blaring, alone?" he says, and I can tell that he's mad.

What the heck did I do? "Um, yes," I stumble.

"So you're cured. No more triggers and you didn't think to tell me, or were they never there at all?" I gasp at his accusation. "Did you over exaggerate about your issues?" He takes a step toward me, and I back away from him.

"If you come any closer, I'll slap you," I blurt out and then clap my hand over my mouth at the anger in my voice. That seems to snap him out of whatever funk he has going on because now he just seems hurt. "I'm sorry, I wouldn't hit you. I just... I can't believe you'd accuse me of that after you know everything."

"Fate, I'm sorry. I didn't mean it. There is just shit going on with the band and the tour. When I came home and heard the music blaring and opened the door to a dark apartment, I panicked. Then to see you just sitting on your bed reading in a barely lit room with the music, I just..." He smacks his hand down on my desk and I don't move a muscle. "I'm an asshole, I'm sorry."

"Do you really think I'd do that? Lie about all of my struggles. I thought you knew me," I whisper, and his face scrunch up in agony.

"Of course not. I'm just a damn idiot. When did this happen?" he says, turning toward me.

"You left. I didn't have anyone to do baby steps with, so I did them by myself. Step by step until I was in my bed with just that lamp and your music." He flinches, and I'm not sure what is bringing him such distress. "Are you mad?" I don't know why he would be; I haven't done anything wrong.

"Well, no, of course not, but after being gone and coming back home to find the girl I love having made all these steps without me kind of sucks," he says laced with sarcasm.

I don't know why, but I snap. "You have no right to be acting this way. You left. What am I supposed to do, stay scared and wait for you to come home and let you save the day?" I shout.

"No," he roars and takes a step forward. Instead of stepping back like I usually would, I step forward, meeting his anger. "I didn't leave you. You're making it sound worse than it is. It was work. I asked if you wanted to go see Clarissa, you didn't have to stay here alone."

"I shouldn't have had to go see Clarissa. You should have wanted me to go with you," I scream, and his face turns from anger to surprise.

"Fate, I didn't—"

"Don't! I don't want a stupid excuse. You can do things on your own just like I can. You went and worked, but so did I. This was what I did. It's a step, that's all," I say while trying to calm myself.

"Fate, I didn't think you'd want to come because of all the media stuff. That's why I never asked you, because I didn't want you to come just for my sake. I missed the hell out of you. It was the worst time." He sighs. "The whole time I was thinking about coming home to you. I swear to you, not asking you to come wasn't because I didn't want you there or so I could do something without you. I want to do everything with you and be a part of your life and you mine. That's why I got so mad, because I saw you did this without me, and it made me feel like you didn't need me."

The Cameron before me isn't one full of anger but one showing me all his vulnerabilities. "Cameron, no. I do need you. So much so that I'd be lost without you. Yes, I did this, but there were so many things I couldn't do while you were gone," I say, holding my hand out for him to take. He doesn't hesitate when he does. It's like my Cameron is back. The distance is gone and we are 'us' again.

"I couldn't sleep during the night without you here. So I went back to my old ways. I slept during the day with all the lights on. Without you that is all I could do. Just enough to keep me charged, no more than that. I couldn't sleep for hours without waking. It was like before I met you again. Does that sound like someone who doesn't need you?" I ask, and he shakes his head, staring deep into my eyes. "Don't you dare say I do not need you. Never say that," I say, hoping he will see I'm just as vulnerable here.

"I'm sorry, Fate. I didn't know. You should have told me. Never again, okay? If I go, then you go too," he says, and I nod. "I have to shower before we go to bed. I smell like smoke, and I know how much you hate that. Want to join me?" he says with a cocked eyebrow.

"Nice try, Cameron. Get your butt in the shower,

I have some reading to do," I say, but I know I have something else I need to do. He gives me a quick kiss before leaving me alone in my bedroom. Once the sound of the shower starts I pick up my phone and go to the drawer in my desk, pulling out one of the cards I'd placed in there. Quickly, I dial the number and she answers on the first ring. "Regina Ryle."

"Hello, Regina, it's Fate McKenzie."

"Hello, Fate, I hoped I'd hear from you. Does this mean you've reconsidered my offer?" she asks, hopeful.

"Yes, I can meet you tomorrow at four." She is ruffling papers and I wait the whole time, holding my breath. I hope she is available then because it is a time I know I can get away from Cameron.

"I have to switch a couple things around, but I can do that." She gives me an address to meet her at. Just like that, it's done and I'm off the phone.

I'm finally going to do it. Grabbing my phone, I decide I should probably make sure nothing new is leaked out to the media. Staring down at the headline, my heart is destroyed by what I'm reading. *A Change in Fate*, it reads, and under it, a picture of Cameron kissing Trisha.

Chapter Thirty-Two

Fate

"How could you? This is what you call work?" I say as I confront him as he steps out of his bedroom after he got dressed. I can't even hold the tears in. I finally let them out as my walls come crashing down around me. Cameron just stares at me. He seems to have no idea what I'm talking about. I toss my phone at him as I walk to my room. He isn't long behind me and I know he's watching me from the doorway as I start packing up the rest of the boxes from us having to move out of the apartment. "We were supposed to be moving into a house together, and you were kissing another girl. Worst of all, her. I knew something happened when we fought about the media coverage, and you left me to go to California. Then you think I'm lying to you. Maybe that's because you were lying to me. Now this comes out. It all makes sense."

Cameron just stands there speechless, but not at all surprised by what he has in his hand.

"Tell me it's an old picture. Tell me she set you up again to look like a big stupid idiot. Please, for our *'forever in a day,'* tell me you didn't throw all that away, me away, for her."

He shifts his feet and I gaze into his eyes. He appears to have tears he's holding back. "It was a set up." My heart begins to steady, but it's only momentarily safe. "She set it up for her to bump into me after the incident with you being hounded by the media. She wanted to discredit you. So when she did it, I saw the cameras and I let it happen." I break out in a full sob, and my body is shaking. Cameron reaches for me, and I slap him away from me. "Don't you get it?" he says loudly. He goes again to reach for me, and I push him back hard. "Fuck! I did this for you," he roars, and I don't flinch. I stand there strong as my heart is being crushed.

"Don't. You. Dare."

"Fate. I was watching it tear you apart with all the shit they were saying about you in the papers. All the questions about your dad, and I know you were hurting. Did you want me to let it continue till it broke you and I had to commit you like Clarissa did?"

I can't help the gasp that comes from me. He is using that as a reason for all this.

"So, I made them leave you alone. I gave them what they wanted, the bad boy rock star, instead of them focusing on the girl who changed me. But you did change me. I love you." His words make me want to throw up. The emptiness of my room is telling me that everything is happening for a reason here.

"You love me? If this is what love is, then you can keep it. I. Don't. Want. It," I say in disgust.

"Don't say that," he begs.

"I didn't change you, you can't be saved," I say and I regret the last part, but it slips out and there is no going back.

"I did change," he roars. "Before you I would have

just let the media eat up anyone who was keeping the heat off of me. Instead, I gave up everything we have worked on to get my image clean again to protect you. Don't you get that?"

"You're right," I say, and he appears hopeful. "You gave up everything we had worked on for this shit. I will never trust anyone again."

"It meant nothing, Fate. I was wishing she was you the whole three damn seconds. I didn't kiss her with anything in me. I made sure they got the picture and I was out of there. I didn't even wait to explain to Trisha how her plan backfired and I used her."

He is making it sound so rational and I want to believe him. I want to trust this, but knowing he touched her again is like a knife to my chest. "You don't get it. We can't just be together. They have more fuel for the fire now. You've made me out to be an idiot. They even used my name against me. The name my mother gave me because I was her 'fate,'" I say, reminding him of my hurt.

He cringes and I know he's feeling this too. "I didn't think," he says.

"That's your problem, Cameron, you don't think. You just do. That's not what a relationship is. I was actually going public. I have an interview tomorrow so I could put it to rest. I was going to be open about my past and everything so they would stop digging and leave us alone. So we could have our happy ending, but because of you, I don't get one." My sight is blurry from the tears that just can't seem to escape fast enough.

"You were going to go public about what your dad did?" he says, holding back a sob.

"Yes, I was. You gave me that strength, and I wanted

this enough to show the world you were that important to me. That's what you do when you feel that way about someone, but I was so wrong," I whimper. The agony my words are bringing to him is breathtaking. I don't use the word love. I can't, and he just gave me one more reason to keep it to myself.

"Fate, please, I am so sorry. You're right, I should have come to you. I just wanted to protect you from it all." Tears are rolling down his face, and it takes everything in me not to go to him. He has ruined every moment with him right now because I doubt his words, his love.

"This is why I kept pushing you away." This was it, my fate was to be burned. "I told you I was like a moth to the flame, and you just burned me, Cameron. There's no going back from this," I say because I just can't see a way around this. He was willing to let her come between us again after he swore it would never happen.

"There has to be some fish fact or logic to prove this can be whole again. Something that can heal the burned pieces," he says, and my mind is a mess.

There are ocean plants that help with inflammation and other medical drugs, but I'm giving him no help in this. We are not an ocean with all its wonders. We are just Cameron and Fate. Well, we were. We will never be that again.

"This is not the end. There is no end for us. *'Forever in a day.'* Forever, that's fate," he pleads.

"Our *'forever in a day'* has passed. Those days are over, Cameron. I can't trust you. I don't trust her, and she's everywhere. She will always be in our way. This will always haunt us." My words bring both of us pain and this needs to end. We are only hurting each other. He'd be better off without a girlfriend with my history in his life. It could come up any time and I know I still haven't come to terms with it in this moment, so he will always worry for me. What will that worry make him do? Something like this. I just can't do this again. The more I'm with him, the more I need him, and I already will be broken without him. I'm barely able to catch my breath, but if I let him in again I might not even have that strength if something happens.

"You don't have to do this. I love you, Fate," he declares, and I let it sink in one more time that I have been truly loved by this man but the world just doesn't want to give us our forever. No, that's all gone. All I have is an empty heart.

"You can't," I implore.

"I love you, Fate, please hear me," he pleads.

"No, that's not possible because I'm all used up. I'm unlovable," I say, speaking from my heart. I have nothing left to give him. Why won't he believe me?

"Stop saying that," he yells at me while grabbing me and pulling me into a passionate kiss.

My body gives in because my heart is telling it this is the last time. When I can pull away I place my hands on his chest, lightly pushing us apart. "That doesn't change the fact that you've broken my heart. I need you to leave. I can't do this right now."

Watching him walk out that door is like a ton of bricks being dropped on my heart. I want to call Clarissa and tell her everything, but I need to figure this out for myself first. It's time I find my own strength and stop depending on others to help me figure out my life.

I keep going back to everything he said. I know he thought he was doing the right thing. He was trying to protect me. I can't say that he hasn't always tried to do that. Unfortunately, while doing that he hurt me worse than the thing he was trying to protect me from. I'm not just losing Cameron here. Scott and Cecilia will be cut from my life too, but nothing compares to the empty feeling of knowing I have to move on without Cameron. *Move on?* That's ridiculous, I won't move on. I can't. He's made that impossible. No one will ever measure up to the peace he brought me and no one will be able to take the pain away from the loss of him. I keep playing his words over in my head, and I want to believe them. 'You don't have to do this, Fate, I still love you.' Could it be that easy?

It took hours, but my willpower wavered. I should have trusted him and not jumped to conclusions. I pick up the phone and call him, because I made a promise that if I thought I should run after him that I would. Now, I just worry he won't take my call. It rings a few times before he answers, but then all that pain I was feeling disappears. Cameron, my Cameron picked up my call. Then that voice is in the background. *Trisha.* I can't hear what exactly she is saying, but I know it is Trisha. There she is, always getting in our way again. The pain comes crashing back but this time there is no hope.

"Fate," he says, and my world is torn apart just by

the sound of the pain in his voice. He's hurting too, but he's not alone. I'm here barely breathing.

"I'll be gone by the time you get back. So this is our goodbye, Cameron, have fun with your friend."

Chapter Thirty-Three

Cameron

CLICK.

"Are you listening to me? I will not be used to make it easier for her. I'm supposed to be the one you're with," Trisha's screeches grate over my nerves like squeaky chalk on a blackboard.

"Trisha, I don't have time for this shit. I'm only here to tell you that I will not be seeing you again. You won't be at shows. If we are at the same party, you will stay away from me. I do not want you around me." My heart is racing. I have to get to Fate. Damn it, I screwed up again, now she thinks I ran off to Trisha. My girl is hurting, and I don't care if Trisha is okay with our arrangement of her staying out of my life. "I have to get to Fate and fix this shit that you've done."

"Oh no, don't blame me. This is on you too," Trisha says, and I know she's right. I let her do this. "The best part is you played the game for me, I didn't even have to really lift a finger. You screwed your little Fate all by yourself." Her words are full of venom, and I pull back from the sting. "I knew once I saw who she was it would only be a matter of time before you screwed it up. I figured you'd come back, but now I can just go to the press and play the victim card. You brought me into your mess, and I'm going to use it to my advantage."

"Cecilia has wanted to kick your ass from day one, and I'll let her. I'll even pay for her bail to get her out." Turning, I run out the door.

"She will never take you back now," Trisha yells from behind me.

Rushing into our apartment, her lights are still on, and I run inside. She is pulling items into her backpack and all her stuff is packed and labeled. Not for our place. Clarissa's address written across the boxes and that burns me.

"Crap," she says when she sees me there. "I thought you'd be longer with your 'friend.' I must have interrupted near the end for you to make it here in time. You didn't have to stop on my account." The fact that she is even thinking I was sexual with Trisha makes me want to puke. Does she not get I don't want to touch anyone but her?

"I wasn't screwing her." She cringes and continues putting the rest of her things away. "I told you, I haven't been with her like that. I've only been with you since the day you changed my world and told me to get my shit together. You're all I ever want. I have no need to go to someone else. I love you. You have my heart and it is always going to be with you."

"So we fight and you run off to Trisha. Explain it to me if it isn't what I'm thinking."

My girl is standing before me, giving me a chance, but all I can think about is her call. "Tell me why you called me," I say in response, and her face turns to surprise. She wasn't expecting me to ask her that instead of pleading my case.

"It doesn't matter," she replies.

"Why did you call me, Fate?" I ask, penetrating her with my stare.

"To say goodbye," she whispers, and I'm enraged.

"Bullshit." This is what she does, she hides and I let her. It has to stop sometime or we will never get past this.

"Why did you go to Trisha?" she asks, and I give her this. Maybe it will be enough to break down those walls again.

"I went there to set things straight. She wasn't happy to find out I used her to make your life better, but I told her I never want to see her again. Not at shows or parties. I'm done, and she has to accept that or I will make her life very difficult." Fate just nods her head as I talk and those walls are there as strong as before. "She will never come between us. I've seen to that," I tell her, hoping she understands that I mean it. It's Fate and I against the world, whatever world she wants to live in, I'll give it to her. A life outside of the public eye or one in the spotlight, I don't care.

"It's not just her, it's all of this. Some things just can't be conquered."

Her words knock the wind out of me. *How can she feel like that? I know she loves me. She has to, right?* Turning away from her, I don't even hold back. My fist crashes into the door with a loud bang, and she yelps. Resting my head against the door, I think back, searching for something, anything to make this girl stay here. To have her let me love her unconditionally, but I don't know how to do that, and it only further infuriates me. All I can remember are our baby steps. Every touch.

Every moment of progress for us, for herself, but most of all for me as well. This girl made me come undone and she built me back up again. I was this person who had guilt over my mother, issues with judgment because I judged myself the worst, and I had no idea how to love. Then Fate walked into my life and blew me out of the damn water. She consumed my body and soul. She began haunting me and my music. Fate was everywhere, and I just know there isn't a way to change that for me, I'm in far too deep.

"Cameron," she whispers and brings me back home. Not home, shit this isn't our home anymore. It's just an empty place full of memories I'd give anything to take with me, but I can't, she won't let me. She's leaving, and I don't know what to do. Music got me through it, but it wasn't a solution. It just got me to Fate. She's my final piece.

"I'll give it all up, be an average person. None of it means anything without you." She just doesn't get it. I decided to do this tour because she wanted me to. She inspired my music again, and if she's gone, that inspiration goes with her.

"I won't let you do that. I know what music means to you. What about Scott? This is a part of you, Cameron. You can't change that any more than I can change my past. It just can't work. All the cards are stacked against us."

"I don't fucking want it without you, don't you get that?" Holding her hand, I hope my touch can get through to her, but she just lets her hand drop from mine.

"You've put your world on hold for me enough. I can't and won't ask you to do that anymore," she states, and I just feel like it's a lost cause. My only chance is to make her realize she can be normal. Have it all, love and all those words that go with it.

"Why did you call me tonight, Fate?" I'm pleading with her.

"I told you, Cameron. To say goodbye." Her words sound like they are coming from another person. Someone I don't even know.

"You are such a damn liar, Fate." She gasps at my candor, but it's now or never. "You're just scared, that's okay. I'm scared too. You have no idea how scared I've been at times. I know you love me, and it's okay to be scared by that."

"I..." She stops and just shakes her head.

"Say it. Don't go about it in a roundabout way. Either you do or you don't. Tell me you love me, Fate," I say, hoping she will finally be able to tell me how she feels. We could move on from all this damn bullshit and have the rest of our lives to continue loving each other.

"You know I can't..." she cries.

"Yes, you can. If you love me, you can tell me. I can. I love you, Fate." I pull her hand in mine. "See, it wasn't hard because it was true. Say it, Fate." I need this from her.

"I'm sorry," she says, and I let go of her hand.

"Then go," I say, and she flinches. *Isn't that what she wants?*

"Cameron."

"You know I love you too much to let you walk away, but I need this. Tell me you love me, Fate. Make it so I can breathe again because I can't come back knowing you will be here at school. I can't watch you be in my world and not love you." This girl just blew up my world and now I have to deal with her coming back here. Being whole without me.

"I won't come back."

Just like that, I have nothing left. Watching her take off her necklace and place it on the table, my world ends. I thought having her in my world would be the death of me, but not having her at all is worse.

"I'll move so far away that I won't even cross your mind. Do what you have to so you can leave me behind." Her words are like the final nail in my coffin. "This place no longer feels like home."

She grabs her backpack and small suitcase before she goes to walk out of her room. She will never be back here again and that is agony. We aren't leaving here to move to our new life, a new apartment, and our forever. None of that exists anymore. She stops in front of me and her raise her hand to touch my face.

"Don't, please," I beg. "If you're just going to say goodbye, then don't." She pulls her hand way from me and I know this is it. I just lost Fate.

Chapter Thirty-Four

Fate

LYING ON MY BED at Clarissa's house, the wetness of my tears is soaking into my pillow. A hundred times I thought about not getting on that plane, but here I am back in the city I was living in before Cameron came smashing into my world. That night when I left, I thought I was feeling complete agony, but nothing compares to this. The longer I'm away from him the harder it is for me to breathe. I keep thinking that at any moment I'll take my last breath because the pain is too much for my heart and soul to handle.

A part of me knows I did what I needed to do. I couldn't be the girl of his dreams. I'm not someone who should be on the arm of a rock star, but I also know that because of him I will never be on the arm of anyone. Cameron McAlister decimated me with his love. There isn't a do-over here. No way could anyone love me as intensely as he did. Another part of me wishes I could go back to that room and give him everything he needed from me.

"Fate, are you sure about this?" Clarissa whispers as if she's scared I'm going to go off the deep end at any moment.

"I didn't have a choice. He deserves someone who can love him without fear of the words and everything being in it brings. He deserves to be loved, Clarissa."

"And you don't?" she asks, and I just turn away from her. "Are you sure you don't, or can you just not say I love you? It's okay to not be able to say it after everything you've been through. I love you, and I know you love me without you having to tell me. You show me, that's enough for me." She brings her hand up, wiping some tears from my cheek and there's nothing. No flinch, no pain, but even worse, no warmth.

"He was right. I really am the ice princess," I blurt out, and I groan in frustration when Clarissa gasps.

"Fate, why would you say that, but better yet why would he?" She glances over at my empty walls and the room appears as if I'm just here temporarily.

I haven't unpacked. I couldn't. The memories are far too fresh. I don't know if I will ever be able to confront those memories of Cameron. Once I do, that's it. Those are all I have left of him. The memories: our beautiful baby steps and all our touches. "It's the truth. I thought he'd melted it all away." Using Cameron's words brings immense suffering to my soul. "I was wrong. All he did was stand on the outside peeking in. I couldn't let him in all the way. He needs more than I have to offer him."

"Are you sure about that? Is this about what you think he wants or did he actually say that?"

My mind goes back to that night and I wonder if I'd begged him to just give me time to work through the chaos if he let me stay. "He told me to leave if I couldn't say I loved him." Her expression would break my heart if it were possible to break an already destroyed heart. I can tell she is feeling my pain too.

"People say stupid things when they are scared. I bet if you called him he'd answer and you could talk this all through."

She doesn't seem to get that this isn't something I haven't already thought about. Every day I sit here thinking about just calling him and explaining everything. "He hasn't contacted me, Clarissa." The discomfort from that is disastrous.

"How could he? When you moved back here you got a new local number, and I got a new house since he was here. Maybe he is hoping you will reach out to him," she says hopefully.

"He's a rock star, Clarissa. If he wanted to find me, he could. It's not like I'm hiding." She lets out a sigh, and I hate that I'm fighting her so much on all this but sugar-coating it isn't going to help me now.

"You left. Maybe he thinks you don't want him to come for you. Rejection can be a horrible thing even for a rock star, Fate. He also knows everything about you. I'm sure he's worried he would just make things worse for you if the feelings are unrequited."

"Clarissa, it's been two months. He has moved on." *Please don't be in love with someone else.* My heart is unbelievably torn. My mind is made up. I can't love him until I can love myself.

"You don't know that."

"I told him to. Finally, I succeeded in pushing him away."

"Fine, but you can't just lock yourself in here. You've done that long enough, and I don't want you doing that again." She tries to pull the covers from me, but I hold them tightly.

"I can't, please don't make me. It's still so raw," I say honestly, because the loss is exactly that.

"If it hurts this much, maybe you should go to Cameron. Take the chance he wants you to. Let him love you."

That would just be too easy. When I got back here, I could feel it. He wasn't the problem. I was. I'm broken beyond repair. "That's just not in the cards for my life." I sigh.

"Life is too cruel, without love there would be no reason to live it."

Her words pull on my soul. "Clarissa, I just can't. Please drop this," I beg her.

"Fine, you're home now, we will work this all out." Her fake enthusiasm only makes me feel worse.

"But it doesn't feel like home anymore. Nowhere does," I say to Clarissa and I'm sure this hurts her, but I know she understands my home was with Cameron.

Clarissa leaves me to dwell, but it isn't long before she is knocking on my door again. "Fate, something came in the mail for you." Walking over to me, she hands me the envelope and I put it on my nightstand. "Don't you want to open it?" she asks, and I just shake my head.

"Doesn't matter what's inside. It can wait." Honestly, I don't care what it is because it's not what I want. It's not Cameron. He is off being a rock star again, and I'm back where I started. My father is gone, finally out of my life but, of course, not forgotten. He still haunts me, and Cameron is off showing the world how talented he is.

"I think you'll want to open this," she states, handing

it back to me and leaving me alone in my room.

I go to put the envelope back down but something makes me change my mind. I open it, pull out a magazine and spot a note stuck on the front of it.

You should read this. If you don't, you're fucking stupid. P.S. I miss you.

Another sticky note marks a page, and I flip to it. My heart sinks as I stare down and tears drop onto the pages below. There before me is Cameron. It's an interview he did for this month's edition. Reading through it, it's like I'm there with him.

This week I got to sit down with none other than lead man, Cameron McAlister from Ten Ways Gone, who are currently on tour. They are also writing songs for their new album that will be released in the fall. Cameron wanted to get down to business right away, jumping in to talk about all the media coverage issues and his image.

This past year he has been attending school at the University of Pennsylvania. Even though the rocker tried to deal with his image issue, there were still some speed bumps. He was, at the time, dating Fate McKenzie, whom he'd met while enrolled at the university. They kept their relationship quiet for privacy reasons, but unfortunately, when he was arrested for assaulting her father, news broke of his new relationship resulting in pictures of them being leaked. The charges where eventually dropped but the media frenzy did not stop as rumors came up that her father was a registered sex offender.

Sources close to the couple say the father had served time. Miss McKenzie hadn't been involved in her father's life since she was a young child, but the rumors of him abusing her were brought into speculation, although nothing has been confirmed. When asking Cameron about Fate's relationship with her father, all he would tell us was that it was her story to tell and that they were not close. He spoke about his issues with anger that had contributed to the altercation between his then girlfriend's father and himself, stating that he regrets his actions but not the passion behind them. He continued to say that Fate was a key player in him being able to get a handle on his anger.

He talked in depth about the incident with Trisha Hanley, who would not comment when we reached out to her. Cameron stated that the picture that was leaked to the media was set up by Trisha herself to cause issues in his relationship with Fate. He went on further to say that Trisha has no place in his life. We asked if he indeed kissed her and his response was one we weren't expecting. Cameron stated he pushed her away as soon as the photo was taken. He let this happen to protect Fate, who was struggling with being hounded relentlessly by the media covering his relationship. His hope was that if they had something else to talk about they might leave them alone. However, he disclosed to us that this was, in fact, the reason behind their final argument. He set the record straight, and when asked why he thought Fate would be okay with this, he continued to call himself a variety of expletives. He is still our bad boy at some level, but I can tell you, after my interview, there is no doubt that he loves Fate McKenzie.

Our question is, has their fate already been sealed or can they make this work? When asked about the possibility of getting back together, Cameron went on to say that he was not the one behind the break-up, if you could call it that. To him, this is very much still real and he understood her reasons, but in his mind, they were still very much the real deal. During this interview, I noticed that he was holding a *heart pendant in his hand. When asked about the pendant he stated it was special to him. He went further to say that you may be able to get rid of physical things, but words remain etched in your soul. This interviewer asked him to clarify, and he said sometimes it's not about having to choose. He continued to say that he holds no hard feelings toward her and only wishes her happiness.*

At the end of the article, there is a tiny heart. Cecilia has written something. *Looks like I'm not the only one who misses you.*

This only furthers my torment because I know I'm still the problem between us, and I haven't dealt with that yet. Then I think of something crazy, but it's the only chance I have.

"Clarissa," I call out, and she comes running to the door. "There's something I have to do."

Chapter Thrity-Five

Fate

"YOU'RE NOT REALLY THINKING this through, Fate," Clarissa says, and I know she is worried about me. She's a mom to me, and having your child in this situation is never something you would support. I know I'd be having the same trouble driving my daughter to this meeting.

"I have to, Clarissa." I need to see this through.

"You don't. This won't fix it."

I know what she is referring to, but I can't go there. I keep my walls in place. "I can't talk about this right now, Clarissa," I snap back. Her face turns from worry to sadness; I immediately regret my words. "I'm sorry. I just...I have to end this today. Living with the fear is killing me from the inside out."

When we pull up outside, I know she wants to come in with me. She turns off the car and the memories are trying to break through. I stay strong. She gets out and comes around to open my door. She takes a deep breath and glances down at me. "Are you ready for this?" I shake my head and her grip on the door tighten. "I'd kill him, you know, to keep you safe."

"I know, and that's why I can't let you come in there

with me. You will protect me, and this is something I have to do on my own. It's time I take my life back." She nods, and I get out of the car and walk into the building, never taking a breath until I'm finally through the doors.

Standing in the waiting room, the terror starts to take hold of me. *Breathe, Fate, you can do this.* The bell sounds, startling me. An announcement is made, telling visitors to make their way to the visitation area. The dread is overwhelming. I walk to the gate and give my ID to the man. He points me in the direction of the visitation area. When I walk through the door, the glass windows send chills down my spine and my breath becomes uneven. I sit in my chair as I wait for this moment.

As he sees me come into his sight, the smile that comes to his face sickens me. He picks up the phone on his side of the glass, and I slowly grab mine. As soon as he speaks, I regret being here. "My baby girl couldn't stay away, she needed her daddy."

All those feelings I have been holding in come out, not in tears but in the anger I have never been able to show him. "I'm not your baby girl. You lost that right when you snuck into my bedroom after Mom died. A father doesn't do what you did to his daughter. You don't deserve that name. The only reason I kept Fate was for Mom, she wanted that to be my name. Always telling me it was her fate to be my mother, but your name, I gave that up as soon as I could. I will *never* be your daughter again," I say venomously.

He doesn't flinch. He just appears stunned. "You can't change blood. You can never change that," he finally says, and I'm already shaking my head in response.

"I can't change the fact that you had a part in my coming into this world, but you were the reason I hid in this world for so long. What happened, why then? You never came to my room before," I ask because it's a question I have been asking myself since that morning I woke up and my whole world had changed.

"After your mother died...I was lonely."

Bile burns at the back of my throat. I only hope I don't vomit. "How dare you? Don't use Mom. If anything, I think the only reason was because you know Mom would have killed you before she let you touch a child. Because, Kurt, I was just a child. You took that from me. I lost Mom and, just like that, I lost my father too. The damage you did in those nine months after Mom was gone will be with me for the rest of my life. You are sick. I hope they keep you in here for a very long time, so you can't ever do this to another child."

"It was only you, Fate. I never did this before that night." He actually seems as if he's struggling to talk. "The following morning I felt sick to my stomach for what I did to you. I swore I'd never do it again, but every time I got back into the booze I found myself back in your room. Each time, I said the same thing until I knew it was no use, I'd do it again. Then I became addicted to it. To that fear I got from you. I never thought you'd tell anyone."

If it hadn't been for Clarissa, he probably would have never been caught. She just reminded me so much of my mom, and when she stood in front of me asking me to let her help, I believed her. "You destroyed me," I whisper.

"There isn't a day that goes by that I don't know

that. When they took you from me, I was actually relieved. I knew you'd be taken care of better than I could ever do myself. Your mother was my glue. She kept me in line and without her I had to find my own way. I was in a treatment program when I saw you in the tabloids and all over the Internet, and it was like I was back in that house again."

"I'm not yours. I never was. I *was* your daughter. The job you had was to protect me and you failed to protect me from you. The one person I shouldn't have had to worry about. I'm studying Law. I'm going to do this not to defend people like you but to make sure they pay for their crimes. So know that if you ever come near me again, I will have you thrown right back in here." I pause, giving him a moment to get his thoughts in order. I know he won't willingly agree to this.

"You could come to some of the meetings, and we could work it out. I could be your dad again." His words only reinforce that this man is truly sick, he's all over the place and can't seem to figure out that this isn't a second chance for our family, it's the final straw.

"That's never going to happen, Kurt. If you don't stay away, you know you will end up back in here or dead," I threaten. "I may not be able to do it, but Clarissa already wants you dead and Cameron...I'm sure if given the chance you'd be gone. Take this as what it is, a goodbye."

"I know you're not together anymore, even in here I have ways of checking in on you."

The pain he brought me as a child was horrendous, but nothing compares to the pain of what it's like with Cameron gone. Sometimes things just don't work, no matter how much you want them to. Some people are just too damaged to get through things like this. "Don't," I plead, and it flashes back to that night with Cameron asking me the very same thing, begging me to stop this. My heart feels as if it's being torn into pieces and then set on fire. All that's left of us is the ashes, and they're being blown away. My time with him is gone. The walls I've been keeping up since I was a child come crashing down. All those moments with Cameron flash before me and each one is like a knife to my heart. All the things, the good and the bad, I just can't forget Cameron. He tried to keep me there, but all I did was run away.

"I have no right to give you advice, but I am begging you not to let what I did ruin your life. I think about your mother and me…" Kurt pauses and tears are cascading down his cheek. I have never seen my father cry. "I'll see her one day, and she will hate me for the pain and devastation I have given our child. Don't let me ruin you forever. I know she's here watching over you. I beg you…" His words are shaky and he is sobbing. "Don't let the actions of a monster control you. If you do, you're nothing like your mother. She didn't let me consume her." With his words, I wonder if my mother ever saw such a hateful side of this man. My heart hurts. She never showed anything, she was so strong. "If I get out and I go back to the booze… If I find you, I'm sorry. As long as I'm sober I will never bother you again, and I hope they keep me in here. I hope they keep this monster in its cage." This is a piece of the father I saw before my mom died. Mental illness and addictions can change people.

"You won't find me. I'll make sure of it. I don't know what it feels like to be you, Kurt. I won't ever know that feeling. I hate you, my own father. But I will also say thank you. If you hadn't come back and shown me that I had to find my own strength, I'd probably be hiding for the rest of my life. I'm done hiding. Do you hear me? I never want to see you again. This ends now." The force in my voice is something I've never experienced before and by the expression on his face he knows I'm serious.

"You can't change history. I wish you could."

His words are true. My walls are finally coming down around me again. "But I can change *fate*." Walking out, I finally feel free.

Chapter Thirty-Six

Cameron

"I THINK YOU SHOULD start off with that new song, just come out of the dark like you've been practicing," Cecilia says, and the pain of having to go out and sing without Fate in my life is too much to bear. What the hell was I thinking when I let her go? She couldn't say it, and I pushed her right out the door. I called her phone after I finally got my head out of my ass, but she'd changed her number. My mind is screaming at me, calling me every name in the book.

Going to Clarissa's is an option as I saw the address on the boxes before the movers got them, but she changed her number. That was enough to tell me she didn't want me to find her. She has gone home. Our apartment is bare and empty since we both moved out for summer break, but my heart feels as if I left it in that room. When she left I felt like I couldn't damn breathe. For two months I've felt nothing but the loss of Fate. Every night I'm dragged into the nightmare of a world with her walking away. At least in there I don't tell her not to touch me, but when she does, the gesture is empty. It's a new form of punishment. I regret not letting her touch me one final time before I lost her forever.

"I can't, Cecilia, it's too soon. You know what that shit is about. How in the hell do you think I can go out there and sing about it so soon? What if I lose it there on stage?" She just stares at me, shaking her head. This girl can drag me over the rocks, something she picked up on from Fate, but I can't handle this right now. Each moment unto the next is torture. Breathing without her is painful enough. She got angry with me, and I did what I do best. I screwed up. When she called and I wasn't alone, I felt my damn body break and the only repair is Fate. I had her, and that's all that should have mattered. The words I needed to hear were just words, her actions were everything I should have needed and more, but I pushed her.

"Didn't you always say to our girl that hiding doesn't help anyone?"

I glance at her and tears stinging the back of my eyes. "Using my own words against me, that's fucking low, Cecilia," I spit out in anger.

"Fine, you want to get angry, get angry, but go out there and show them you feel. That she melted the ice away from our rock star. She made you real and, for heaven's sake, since you won't listen to your own words, maybe you will listen to what she used to say. Go out there and say, 'screw it, world, I'm here'."

Those words ruin me. A train wreck against my chest would have been less impactful than those five words, and Cecilia damn well knows it. "If I get called a pussy tomorrow in the tabloids, I'm going to kick someone's ass, do you get that, Cecilia?"

She just gives me a grin, knowing full well she's succeeded. This girl is the only thing keeping me together, and she's pushing me to move on. That hurts the worst because I know she misses Fate too. "God forbid the rock star gets called names. Don't worry, we will protect your image. I will tell the world I poked you in the eyes before you went out there."

I chuckle at her as the anger I was feeling slips away. She definitely learned that from my Fate. "Why would they believe you did that?" I say, trying to joke with her.

"Because I will tell them you tried to get frisky with me and I, unlike the rest of the world, wasn't interested."

I laugh but at the same time, my soul is being crushed. She's not the only one who isn't interested in me. I all but damn near begged Fate to stay. Screw that, I did beg and still she left me there broken in half.

"It's time to go on, you have this, Cameron."

I stand at the side of the stage; Cecilia is behind the band, watching us. I tell the band the new game plan and then make sure the lights stay off and I take the stage. The crowd is cheering like their life depends on it and my heart is crashing against my chest. You'd think I had never done this before. *Get your shit together.*

The microphone is in front of me and I bring it close to me. The crowd goes dead quiet, waiting for it. "Screw it, world, I'm here," I say quietly, and it comes from the speakers. The whole building to erupt into screams. The dim lights fall on me, but I can't see the crowd. This is the only way I can do this. I can't look into these faces while I say everything I've held back. "This is something I have been working on, and you better fucking like it," I say with the arrogance they are used to getting from me, and they all cheer. "It's called, 'That's Fate,' so here we go." I start playing, and the band picks up. The drums get louder, and the vibrations pulsate throughout my body.

You walked in and I ran out
I thought I was here to save you, but no
Fate saved me and I never got to thank you
The whole time I was wishing she were you
That pain I never want to feel again
Every time you ran away, you took me with you
But not that day you made me stay

My pulse is racing and the crowd is feeding off everything I'm feeling.

So screw it, world, I'm here
Fear me but don't fear Fate
She was brought to us to show us
That we were meant for so much more
Take Fate by the hand and love that girl
If not, you just don't understand
That's Fate

Sometimes Fate is just the most beautiful thing.
Always asking why I love you and need you
Damn that killed me every day
Have you ever loved someone so much it hurt?
I do and I'd destroy anything that tried to harm her
I will stand alone and fight off her demons
That's Fate and I thank God every day

So screw it, world, I'm here
Fear me, but don't fear Fate

She was brought to us to show us
That we were meant for so much more
Take Fate by the hand and love that girl
If not, you just don't understand
That's Fate

The lights come on and, just like that, it happens. Fate is right there in the front row with Cecilia next to her with a shit-faced grin on her face. Glancing back at the guys, I can tell they are just as shocked as I am. The crowd is going insane, and I just see her there so unsure of herself. I see the strength, but my heart is crashing. This must appear final to her, and I just can't let her go without knowing. I focus my eyes on her and continue.

I became the source of her pain
Something I just couldn't bear to be
It was then that Fate was beautifully destroyed
Sometimes she just needs a hand to get through
Let me be that hand and let me just hold you up
Please tell me it's not too late
Tell me Fate hasn't ended here today.

She is pulling up a sign and my heart drops when I read what it says. In big letters, it says Choose. Our code word and this is her saying goodbye, telling me she can't do this but she needs closure.

So I say screw it, world, I'm here
Fear me, but don't fear Fate
She was brought to us to show us
That we were meant for so much more

239

Take Fate by the hand and love that girl
If not, you just don't understand
That's Fate

While I'm singing, she takes the sign down and grab her backpack. The damn pain of it is so much I almost miss a step in my words, but this is the only chance I have to see her. To show her everything I have for her. The crowd is going crazy around her, as they know the closing of the song is coming. The guys go into an instrumental verse. The crowd is trying to catch the beat of this new song and sing with me. All of a sudden, she disappears from the crowd and I can't see her.

I'm frantic when I can't find her walking away. Cecilia's waving her hands and there, just like she always does, Fate shines through with a sign, but this time it says something different. Her lips moving, and I know without having to read it what she's saying. Tears creep into my eyes, and I need to get to her. I signal the guys to keep the instrumental going, and I walk to tell the security at the front of the stage to get Fate. When she is at the end of the stage, I put my guitar behind my back and pull her up. She steps back, holding the sign now standing in front of me. Staring down, I read the words. 'I choose you, I love you.' She is wearing a Ten Ways Gone Tour T-shirt.

Leaning in, I say loudly, "I have to hear you say it."

She grabs my hand and places it over her heart. God, I've missed her touch. "I love you, Cameron McAlister."

Those words I've been dying to hear from her break me, and I can't hold back. I grab her and my lips crash against hers. Just like that, I'm home again. I can hear the crowd going insane, and she pulls away, hiding her head in my chest. I pull out the thing that has been burning a hole in me since she gave it back.

When she sees it, her eyes light up. She gladly takes her necklace, but she doesn't put it on. She just stares at me for a moment and my heart stops. "Marry me," she says.

I never thought in a million years I'd be happy to hear those words from anyone. But *that's Fate.* Taking her by the hand, I bring her back to the microphone and finish our song. Singing only to her the whole time.

So screw it, world, I'm here to claim her
Fear me, but don't fear my Fate
She was brought to me to show me
That I was meant for so much more
I'm going to take Fate by the hand
Loving you, girl, like you were meant to be
I know what you deserve, and you will make me whole
Because that's our Fate to be.

The End

About The Author

LOOK FOR HER IN the trees enjoying nature's wonders, traveling to see the latest animal conservations, or at aquariums all around the world. This girl loves nature and all animals. She has many pets and is always adding new additions. The more the merrier in her mind. Sitting under the shade reading a book, letting the world around her pass by, while she is safe in her bubble of imagination. Well, that is where she'd love to stay. She is a softball player, can be talked into the occasional Karaoke and loves going out to dance. She is a first generation Canadian living in Ontario. Her family is from Scotland, so finding her in the hot sun for very long is unlikely, but give her rain and thunderstorms and she's golden.

Acknowledgments

I'D LIKE TO DEDICATE this to my friends and family. Those who supported me through this journey and continue to support me. To my loving husband, for every night I've kept you awake with my writing. Each time I hated you because my male character was being an ass. You are the reason I am able to do all of this.

To my family, my little ones. Momma loves you more than anything in this world.

To my best friends Jennifer, Ray, and Cass x 2 ☺ Thank you for being here no matter what else is going on in your lives. You will never truly know how much I adore you all.

Also From Blue Tulip Publishing

BY MEGAN BAILEY
There Are No Vampires in this Book

BY J.M. CHALKER
Bound

BY ELISE FABER
Phoenix Rising
Dark Phoenix
Phoenix Freed
From Ashes
Blocked

BY STEPHANIE FOURNET
Butterfly Ginger
Leave A Mark

BY MARK FREDERICKSON & MELORA PINEDA
The Emerald Key

BY JENNIFER RAE GRAVELY
Drown
Rivers

BY LESLIE HACHTEL
The Dream Dancer

BY CARRIE THOMAS
Hooked

BY NICOLE THORN
What Lies Beneath
Your Heart Is Mine

BY RACHEL VAN DYKEN
Upon a Midnight Dream
Whispered Music
The Wolf's Pursuit
When Ash Falls
The Ugly Duckling Debutante
The Seduction of Sebastian St. James
An Unlikely Alliance
The Redemption of Lord Rawlings
The Devil Duke Takes a Bride
Savage Winter
Every Girl Does It
Divine Uprising

BY KRISTIN VAYDEN
To Refuse a Rake
Surviving Scotland
Living London
Redeeming the Deception of Grace
Knight of the Highlander
The Only Reason for the London Season
What the Duke Wants
To Tempt an Earl
The Forsaken Love of a Lord
A Tempting Ruin
A Night Like No Other
The One

BY JOE WALKER
Blood Bonds

BY KELLIE WALLACE
Her Sweetest Downfall

BY C. MERCEDES WILSON
Hawthorne Cole
Secret Dreams

BY GRACIE WILSON
Beautifully Destroyed

BY K.D. WOOD
Unwilling
Unloved

BOX SET — MULTIPLE AUTHORS
Forbidden
Hurt
Frost: A Rendezvous Collection
A Christmas Seduction

www.bluetulippublishing.com

Made in the USA
Columbia, SC
14 April 2017